DANIEL
X
WATCH
THE
SKIES

Also by James Patterson

THE WOMEN'S MURDER CLUB SERIES

1st to Die

2nd Chance (with Andrew Gross)

3rd Degree (with Andrew Gross)

4th of July (with Maxine Paetro)

The 5th Horseman (with Maxine Paetro)

The 6th Target (with Maxine Paetro)

7th Heaven (with Maxine Paetro)

8th Confession (with Maxine Paetro)

MAXIMUM RIDE SERIES

Maximum Ride: The Angel Experiment

Maximum Ride: School's Out Forever

Maximum Ride: Saving the World and Other Extreme Sports

The Final Warning

Manga Volume 1 (with NaRae Lee)

Max

Manga Volume 2 (with NaRae Lee, to be published November 2009)

DANIEL X SERIES

The Dangerous Days of Daniel X (with Michael Ledwidge)

Daniel X: Alien Hunter Graphic Novel (with Leopoldo Gout)

Daniel X: Watch the Skies (with Ned Rust)

WITCH & WIZARD SERIES

Witch & Wizard (with Gabrielle Charbonnet, to be published October 2009)

ALEX CROSS NOVELS

Kiss the Girls

Along Came a Spider

Cat and Mouse

Pop Goes the Weasel

Roses are Red

Violets are Blue

Four Blind Mice

The Big Bad Wolf

London Bridges

Mary, Mary

Cross

Double Cross

Cross Country

Alex Cross's Trial (with Richard Dilallo, to be published September 2009)

I, Alex Cross (to be published November 2009)

DETECTIVE MICHAEL BENNETT SERIES

Step on a Crack (with Michael Ledwidge)

Run For Your Life (with Michael Ledwidge)

STAND-ALONE THRILLERS

Sail (with Howard Roughan)

Swimsuit (with Maxine Paetro)

NON-FICTION

Torn Apart (with Hal and Cory Friedman)

The Murder of King Tut (with Martin Dugard, to be published August 2009)

ROMANCE

Sundays at Tiffany's (with Gabrielle Charbonnet)

For more information about James Patterson's novels, visit
www.jamespatterson.co.uk

James
Patterson
AND NED RUST

DANIEL
X
WATCH
THE
SKIES

C̲

Century · London

Published by Century, 2009

2 4 6 8 10 9 7 5 3 1

Copyright © James Patterson, 2009

James Patterson has asserted his right under the Copyright, Designs
and Patents Act 1988 to be identified as the author of this work

First published in Great Britain in 2009 by
Century
Random House, 20 Vauxhall Bridge Road,
London SW1V 2SA

www.randomhouse.co.uk

Addresses for companies within The Random House Group Limited can be found at:
www.randomhouse.co.uk/offices.htm

The Random House Group Limited Reg. No. 954009

A CIP catalogue record for this book
is available from the British Library

Hardback ISBN: 9781846054600
Trade paperback ISBN: 9781846054617

The Random House Group Limited supports The Forest Stewardship
Council (FSC), the leading international forest certification organisation. All our
titles that are printed on Greenpeace approved FSC certified paper carry the FSC
logo. Our paper procurement policy can be found at:
www.rbooks.co.uk/environment

Mixed Sources
Product group from well-managed
forests and other controlled sources
www.fsc.org Cert no. TT-COC-2139
© 1996 Forest Stewardship Council
FSC

Printed and bound in Great Britain by
Clays Ltd, St Ives Plc

For Jack, who completes me
—JP

For Ruth, for being proud of me
—NR

DANIEL X

WATCH THE SKIES

Prologue

NIGHT'S WHAT HAPPENS WHEN YOUR SIDE OF THE PLANET IS POINTED AT OUTER SPACE

One

IT WAS A pretty regular early-summer night at 72 Little Lane. The crickets and katydids were making that soothing racket they do on warm, still, small-town evenings. The back porch light was on, but otherwise the tidy brown house was happily, sleepily dark.

At least it was until about eleven thirty, when the dark night in Holliswood became a whole lot darker.

It's hard to exactly translate the command that triggered it—it couldn't be heard by human ears, and the language of insects isn't one that can easily be put into words anyhow—but every six-legged creature in the area instantly hid under rocks, wedged into tree bark, or dug down into the dirt...and became very, *very* quiet.

And then, inside the small brown house, it became very, *very* loud.

Every speaker—on the computers, on the cell phones, on the iPods, on the radios, on the telephones, on the brand-new Sony flat screen with THX surround sound and every other TV set in the house, even on the "intelligent" microwave—began to blast a dance song from a popular old movie.

A song that just happened to be the favorite of a very powerful *alien*.

Two

THE BOY FUMBLED for his clock radio. It was blaring some superlame old seventies song by one of those awful disco bands his mom sometimes played in the car. His sister must have changed the station and turned the volume up full blast as a prank. He'd get her back—later, in the morning, when he'd had some sleep.

He punched the snooze button, but it didn't shut off. He flicked the switch on the side, but it didn't shut off. He picked up the clock from his bedside table and saw that it was just past eleven thirty. She was going to pay for this.

He reached down and pulled the cord out of the socket... *but it still didn't shut off.*

"What the—?!" he said, and rubbed his eyes with his free hand.

The clock's glowing display now read, "DANCE."

And then the disco song started over, and a voice loud and screechy enough to cut through all the noise said: "DO THE DANCE!"

"Now *that's* freaky," said the boy, and just as he started to get *really* scared, a blue spark leaped out of the alarm clock and up his arm—and he bolted out of his room.

He knew what he had to do.

In the hallway he collided with his father but didn't say a word. And now his mom and sister were pushing at him from behind, and the entire family tumbled down the front stairs to the living room.

It was weird, thought the boy, because he was pretty sure he hated dancing.

But now he couldn't stop himself. He strode to the center of the living room and somehow knew exactly what moves to make, and—except for the look of terror in his eyes—he boogied his heart out like a pimply, pajama-wearing John Travolta.

His mom, dad, and sister didn't look like they were having too much fun, either.

In fact, the only fun in the house was being had by the five grotesque alien beings filming the family from behind the eerie lights, high-tech microphones, and multilens video cameras set up in the adjoining dining room.

They were laughing their slimy heads off. Not literally, but if one of these horrific creatures had actually knocked its own block off, picked it up from the floor, and eaten it, the boy wouldn't have been surprised.

"By Antares, they're good," one of the monsters said,

slapping one of its six scaly knees. "It's just like *Saturday Night Fever!*"

And then the fat one in charge—cradling the bullhorn in his left tentacle, nearly crushing the cheap folding canvas chair with his weight—replied with a sigh.

"Yes, it's almost a shame we have to *terminate* them."

Three

THE FIVE ALIENS were still hungry even after their fresh kill. They scuttled and hovered out of the news van they'd swiped from the local TV station and pressed their ugly wet noses against the windows of the Holliswood Diner. A young waitress with wavy black hair was reading a Sherman Alexie paperback at the counter.

"Business is about to pick up *a lot*," said the boss alien, who had a thousand-pound intergalactic champion sumo wrestler's body and the head of a catfish. No ears, no neck, no legs—and no manners.

He reached out to his personal assistant—a big-nosed space ape—grabbed its cell phone, and punched in a number. The three other henchbeasts twitched with anticipation. This was looking to turn into a pretty exciting Saturday night.

When the girl leaned across the counter to pick up the diner's phone, a little spark leaped out of the receiver, arcing straight into her ear. Her eyes turned glassy as she put down the phone and went to open the door for them.

"What did the Zen Buddhist say to the hot-dog vendor?" asked the lead alien as the waitress showed them to their booths, already chuckling to himself at the coming punch line.

"Make me one with everything" said the girl, robotically.

The creatures burst into laughter.

"Actually, on second thought, sweetie," he added, "Why don't you go and make us *everything* with everything. Chop-chop!"

"Good one, boss!" said his assistant, stealthily snatching his cell phone back from where his employer had rested it on the table. He carefully wiped it down with a napkin before putting it back in his purple fanny pack.

The waitress, in the meantime, had flown into motion as if somebody had hit the ×2 button on her remote control. She prepared and delivered to the aliens heaping stacks of eggs, bacon, sausage, waffles, coffee, Cokes, bagels, burgers, turkey platters, meatloaf, mashed potatoes, onion rings, cheesesteaks, cheesecakes, clam chowder, gravy fries, banana cream pies, root-beer floats, and chicken-fried steaks. And several mugs of fryer oil.

"Careful or you'll burn her out, boss," advised one of the henchbeasts.

"Like I care," said the boss. "We got about six billion of

9

them to get rid of. And, come to think of it," he said with a laugh that sounded like somebody blowing bubbles in turkey gravy, "there are plenty more where *you* came from too."

And, with that, he grabbed the henchbeast and pummeled it against the linoleum floor. The sound that filled the diner was like a roach getting crushed by a hard-soled shoe—only much louder.

Four

"THERE'S YOUR DESSERT." The lead alien, who happened to be number five on The List of Alien Outlaws on Terra Firma, gestured at the henchbeast's remains.

The other aliens shared an uncomfortable silence as they slowly converged on the carcass. Number 5 rolled his gooey eyes and continued shoveling fried food into his extrawide mouth.

"Looks like we got company," said the personal assistant, nodding at the flashing red and blue lights in the parking lot. A moment later the front door to the diner flew open, and a sheriff and deputy burst in with their guns drawn.

"Hands u—" the sheriff started to shout, but Number 5 fired a wide-angle ray gun that instantly turned both officers into puddles of something resembling swamp mud.

"Clean that up. I'm eating here," said Number 5.

The two henchbeasts eagerly turned away from the carcass of their fallen comrade and with long, rubbery tongues devoured the human sludge.

"Speaking of annoying law-enforcement types," said Number 5, smacking his lips and sipping a scalding mug of fryer oil, "my spider senses tell me somebody even more pesky is on his way here."

"Not *him*?" asked his assistant.

"The same," said Number 5.

A collective, defensive growl rose up from the alien crew.

"That pipsqueak is *almost* enough to turn me off my Caesar salad," the personal assistant complained, downing an entire bowl of lettuce.

"Let's just remember what's most important here," Number 5 said. "First, keep to the schedule. This is our biggest production yet, and we can't miss a beat.

"And second—ugly as he is—little Danny could very well be our lead man. So let's not kill him ... *right away*."

Part One

ACTUALLY, ALIENS *SHOULD* FEAR THE REAPER

Chapter 1

YOU KNOW THE second-coolest of all my superpowers? It's the one that lets me hear *any* song I've *ever* heard as loud as I want, as often as I want, and anytime I want. It's like I have an iPod implanted in my head. Only it holds, like, *terabytes* more songs, and the sound quality's better. And it never needs to be docked or recharged.

The song I was playing over and over again right then, as I motorcycled down I-80, was "Don't Fear the Reaper" by Blue Oyster Cult. I know it kinda puts the K in Klassic Rock, but it's a good one. And it was going along real well with my thoughts and plans—wherein I am the Grim Reaper...of very, *very* bad aliens.

I leave the good ones alone, of course. But, honestly—not to bum you out—I've only bumped into a couple other "good" aliens here on your Big Blue Marble.

15

So what's the *coolest* of my superpowers, you ask? The way I can smell alien sweat from ten miles away even while speeding along a highway with my helmet on? The way I've recently learned to make high-performance, hybrid-engine racing bikes that can travel three thousand miles at seventy-five miles per hour on a tank of gas? The way I can pop a wheelie...on my *front* tire?

Well, that's almost untopable, but, no, the coolest of my superpowers is the one with which I can create my best friends—Willy, Joe, Emma, and Dana—*out of my imagination.*

It takes some concentration, and I have to be rested and not taking any allergy medicine, but, really, being able to shoot fireballs or outrace locomotives is nothing next to being able to make friends *out of thin air.*

And they're not bottom-of-the-barrel specimens, either. Joe is great with video games and computers, and otherwise is basically a life-support device for the world's fastest-moving mouth. He's either chewing his way through some mountain of food that weighs twice as much as his skinny butt, or he's talking a blue—and totally hilarious—streak.

Emma is our moral compass. The part that gets her worked up about Alien Outlaws is that they're on Terra Firma and doing harm not just to people but to Nature. Mother Earth has no better advocate than her Birkenstock-wearing self.

Emma's older brother is Willy. He's the ultimate wing man, built like a brick and slightly harder to scare than one too. He's our go-to guy when it comes to weapons and engines and stuff like that. Plus, he's more loyal than, like, Batman's butler Alfred, Sam in *The Lord of the Rings,* Wesley in *The Princess Bride,* and King Arthur's horse combined.

Finally, Dana is, well... I guess you could say she's my dream girl. She manages to be both the most attractive and the most grounded person I've ever encountered. In the *universe.* Remember, I haven't exactly been operating out of a Montana shack all these years.

Oh, and all four of them happen to be outstanding at don't-try-this-at-home motorcycle stunts. Which we were thoroughly enjoying on this particular night, chasing after an eighteen-wheeler. Keep in mind that aliens don't necessarily abide by the same rules humans do when it comes to minimum driving age.

"Slalom!" Willy, who was in the lead, called out. One of our favorite tricks.

We leaned the bikes almost on their sides and—get this—zipped *under* the trailer... behind wheels seven, eight, nine, and ten, and in front of wheels eleven through eighteen... and came out safely on the other side.

Finally we pulled up to a small-town diner.

"Sorry about this," I said to my friends, climbing off my bike. I was about to face off with the most powerful alien I'd ever engaged in mortal combat.

"Sorry for what?" asked Joe.

"Number 5," I told them, furrowing my brow. "You smell that?"

There was a terrible smell in the air, like somebody had left a herring-salad sandwich in a hot car... *for a week.*

"Ugh!" Emma wrinkled her nose. "I'm catching it too. Seriously bad news."

"Yeah, Daniel," Willy echoed. "This guy must be more evil than the stink in your sneakers. We better get ready to rumble."

"My sneakers don't smell, Willy," I said. "And I can't put you guys at risk. This is between me... and Number 5."

"You're such a *boy*," said Dana, hand on her hip, a look of concerned disapproval on her face. "Are you sure you're ready to go that high up The List? No offense, Daniel, but you got pretty lucky with Number 6."

"Always with the pep talks, Dana. Thanks a lot."

Then I clapped my hands, and she and the rest of them flickered out of existence. (I actually don't need to clap, but it looks cool.)

And then I cleared my head for battle.

Chapter 2

HIS STENCH WAS bad outside, but that was nothing compared to how it was in the diner. This guy made low tide smell like Obsession for Men.

I must have missed him by just a matter of minutes — the scraps of moist membrane rotting in the booth where he'd been sitting hadn't even skinned over — but he and his henchbeasts had gotten away while the getting was still good.

Unfortunately, with these higher-up-The-List baddies, I was discovering a trend: they often seemed to know I was coming. I guess I should be flattered that they didn't want to run into me, but it was more than a little frustrating to keep bringing my A-game only to find nobody to play with.

Well, *almost* nobody. They'd left behind a waitress.

She was in no shape to play, though. The poor girl was collapsed like a rag doll on the floor next to the counter. Her burnt-out face reminded me of a kid's toy you might have tried to run on a car battery rather than AAAs.

The name stitched on the pocket of her calico uniform was Judy Blue Eyes, and, you guessed it, her eyes were the kind of clear blue a guy could look into and see the promise of the whole world.

A human guy, I mean. For me, the promise of the whole world was usually a great deal darker.

"Hey, Judy. You okay?"

"Nnnn," she said, consciousness slowly percolating back.

I helped her into a booth and gave her a glass of water.

"Wh-wh'appen?" she stuttered.

"Food fight," I said, only it was far worse than that. Smashed china plates, syrup and salt caked on the walls, soda dripping from the tabletops, empty jelly packets stuck to the seats, ketchup and mayo on the jukeboxes, Promise spread splattered on the ceiling, slicks of alien slime pooled everywhere like a sticky mix of spilled honey and coffee.

"Oh gosh," she said, struggling to sit up and take it all in. "I'm *so-o* fired."

"Nah," I said. "I can give you a hand." And then, like somebody had pressed the ×8 button on *my* remote, I zipped around with a broom, a mop, a couple bottles of Windex, and a dozen dishrags and had the place spick-and-span in no time, literally.

"Man, I'm really out of it," said Judy as I returned to her now-gleaming booth. "I mean, did you just clean all that up in, like, ten seconds?"

Man, was she cute. I was trying to think of something clever to say back, but I had this weird—though not totally unpleasant—tightness in my chest, and all I could manage was this really lame giggle.

Must be an alien thing.

Chapter 3

I DON'T KNOW what got into me because it's totally against policy to give the straight scoop to civilians, but Judy insisted on making me a grilled cheese sandwich and a bowl of chili—the aliens hadn't quite eaten *every* scrap of food in the place—and before I knew it I'd told her just about the whole story.

How I was an Alien Hunter and my parents, Graff and Atrelda (bless their weird-named souls), had been Alien Hunters and how their mission was to protect nice folks from the thousands of aliens who wanted to take advantage of, plunder, pillage, and sometimes plain-out destroy places like this.

"Places like this?" Judy smiled wryly, not taking me seriously. "You can hardly blame them for wanting to plain-out destroy Holliswood. I mean, this place is nothing but a prefab smear of parking lots, giant superstores, drive-through banks, twenty-garage automotive franchises, and chain restaurants. And mean girls, dumb jocks, and people who get their news from those scrolly things running across the bottom of their favorite stupid TV show—while running on the treadmill at the gym."

I couldn't help but admire her astute observational skills. Not to mention her honesty, directness...and, okay, cuteness.

"Well, people can't be all that bad here. You're a girl...and you're not mean."

Good one, Daniel. Wish I had Joe's gift of gab. In lieu of that, I kept rambling.

I told her how one of the alien baddies, the worst of the worst, had killed my parents when I was just three, and how I'd barely escaped with my life and—almost as important—The List.

Judy stopped smiling. "Don't joke about your parents being murdered," she said.

"I wouldn't joke about that," I said, wondering if I'd gone too far.

Her eyes were penetrating mine. "And...The List is...?"

There was no stopping the power of Judy's blue eyes, so I spilled all the rest: how The List was, in full, called The List of Alien Outlaws on Terra Firma, and how it was an interactive, constantly self-updating summary of all the ill-intended Outer Ones now residing on the planet, ranked from number one to somewhere in the hundreds of thousands, from most dangerous to those that are barely stronger than a human.

And how my parents' evil murderer—known as The Prayer—was number one on that list...and that it was my life's goal to *hunt him down and kill him.*

Sorry, I get a little hung up on that sometimes.

When I finished, Judy was looking at me like I was C-R-A-Z-Y nuts, so I slapped on my best damage-control smile and said, "Psych! Just messing with you! I love making up stories."

"Oh, sure," she said, blinking her gorgeous peepers and looking more than a little confused—and creeped out.

Sometimes I'm more extrastupid than extraterrestrial.

"Okay, gotta go!" I said, flashing damage-control smile variation number two.

"Sure..." Judy said. "Come back and see us real soon, um—what did you say your name was again?"

"Daniel," I said, and flew out the door before she asked me my last name.

That part of getting to know someone is always a little awkward...when you don't *have* a last name.

Chapter 4

YOU KNOW HOW dogs go wild over mailmen? Well, you haven't seen a dog go *postal* till you've seen one detect the scent of the bad sort of alien. It's hilarious.

Right now, *I* was the one about to go postal because I couldn't detect anything at all. My alien-tracking nose could rival a bloodhound's, but unfortunately, I wasn't getting any directional indications on Number 5. I sensed he was still in town someplace, but he must have started taking some new kind of precautions against me.

I was upset, but not so much that I couldn't recognize it was a beautiful night, and since I needed some rest anyhow, I decided to make camp. I took a minute or two to gaze at the twinkling stars and run through the names of all that were visible. Even on the clearest of Earth nights, you can only see about two thousand stars from the planet's surface...but get me up past the murky atmosphere, and I'll name you a couple million that would be distinguishable even to your human eyes.

Then I turned on my laptop. Not just any laptop, this one—it's one some creatures would, literally, kill for...because it alone contains the complete and perpetually updated List of Alien Outlaws on Terra Firma.

I can shape The List as anything from an interactive scroll to a heads-up display visor, but I usually access it as a laptop, since I like to practice *not* standing out. Plus, that way—when I'm not researching—I can download movies from Netflix.

So I logged in and did a little research on the stinking outlaw I'd just missed at the diner. Number 5 hailed from a remote swamp planet with an unpronounceable name that makes the Siberian tundra seem cosmopolitan.

But since leaving his provincial home and finding his way to the bright lights and big megalopolises of the central star clusters, he'd been working his way through the ranks, and now he was an up-and-coming entertainment mogul. Kind of an alien version of Aaron Spelling, if Aaron Spelling were a few degrees more bloodthirsty than Attila the Hun.

His MO was to find technologically evolving but still largely defenseless cultures—such as Earth's—where he could easily move in, steal some of their better entertainment ideas, enslave their unwary populations, and then walk away with a treasure trove of exploitive, derivative programs that he'd then proceed to syndicate to networks across the cosmos.

So what made this swamp creature worthy of the number five spot on The List? His signature cinematic flourish: to kill his cast as the last act of their skits. In fact, because they always died at the end, he was considered the founder of a new style of alien program that they called—in typically lame alien fashion—*endertainment.*

Nobody's ever accused the Outer Ones of having over-developed senses of humor, that's for sure.

Chapter 5

NOT SURPRISINGLY, AFTER refreshing my knowledge about Number 5, I had some trouble sleeping. Kidnap, brainwashing, wanton murder, callous exploitation of sentient creatures on at least three dozen underdeveloped worlds...

I was going to enjoy removing him from Earth, permanently.

As soon as the sun was up, I headed back to town. Guided by a sort of eighth sense—I have seven legitimate senses, at least that I've so far discovered—that told me there was something funky going on in the immediate vicinity, I pulled into the S-Mart twenty-four-hour super-store and found a parking space next to a minivan that was being loaded by a pregnant woman. She was lifting a flat of motor oil...and sweating like crazy.

"Need a hand with that, ma'am?" I offered. She gave me a blank stare and made a weird bubbling sound with her mouth.

"*Okay,* sorry to bother you," I said, noticing one of her grocery bags seemed to have at least twenty cans of fish food in it. That struck me as a little weird, but maybe she ran a pet store or something.

I turned to go into the store, but as I stepped out from behind the minivan, I almost got decked by a green plastic S-Mart grocery cart—pushed by another pregnant woman.

I did a double take—to make sure I hadn't accidentally wandered toward a Mommies "R" Us or something—and nearly got flattened by *another* pregnant woman, who was seemingly in a race with three *other* pregnant women, all making a beeline for the store's entrance.

"Weird," I said, and headed inside, where things got weirder still.

Chapter 6

I WALKED INTO the store and heard this strange, gurgling voice on the piped-in infotainment shopper channel, and I'm like, huh, *that* sure is a strange person to pick as your announcer. I was relieved to be approached by a very normal-looking, young fresh-faced store clerk as I walked in.

"Can I help you find something, sir?" He looked like a good candidate for Employee of the Month.

"Yeah…" I said, operating on my eighth sense again, "fish food."

As the clerk led me through hardware and housewares and electronics, I found myself gagging. And when I spotted a video display, I understood why.

Scowling on-screen was none other than the unfortunate fish head of Number 5.

And even more unfortunate, *he saw me.*

Number 5 scowled, and his image disappeared, leaving a prerecorded Rosie O'Donnell to talk about some titanium-plated sandwich maker. Maybe he'd spotted me from one of the overhead security cameras. Did that mean he was *in* the store someplace?

"Sir? Are you all right?" the clerk called back to me.

"Couldn't be better," I told him with a weak smile. "Are we there yet?"

"Almost," he replied, as we passed an empty motor-oil section... and then his voice transformed into a hideously twisted gurgle, just like the infotainment announcer's voice: "*We're going to Number 5.*"

I stopped dead in my tracks.

Until I realized that smiley Mr. Employee-of-the-Month was heading toward a sign for *aisle* five — Pet Food. And he was soon surrounded by an enormous throng of pregnant women who stood slack mouthed, staring at some empty shelves where all the fish food had been.

I was just about to tell everyone to take their fish-food orders to a certain minivan in the parking lot, when World War III broke out in aisle four.

Chapter 7

GUIDED BY THE sound of explosions, falling shelves, and screams, I made a mad dash to the source of the chaos, leaping over people, dodging carts, somersaulting over cardboard display stands.

The cause of the commotion was a makeshift film set "manned" by ten henchbeasts that were *melting* terrorized shoppers with their weapons. And heading the group was an alien that made my jaw hit the floor—a big-nosed ape that was none other than number twenty-one on The List.

In hindsight, I probably shouldn't have taken even a nanosecond to think about it. Because as soon as he saw me—and clearly he'd been waiting in ambush—he fired this rifle kind of thing with a round dish on its front end.

At *me*.

I've got some pretty good reflexes, if I do say so myself,

and I managed to leap up into the air before he got the shot off—like high enough so that I could grab one of the exposed I beams in the thirty-foot ceiling—but I wasn't fast enough.

A massive shockwave slammed into me, compressing all the air in the warehouse-sized store and smacking me down like I was a fly and it was a rolled-up newspaper. I crunched onto the floor, my ears ringing, my vision blurry, the room spinning.

"This is gold," Number 21 cackled.

It would've been a great time to conjure up my friends or some weapons to help me kick some alien butt, but right now I could barely remember the word for ouch. I was on my own.

"We've found a lot of talented extras here in S-Mart," Number 21 said darkly. "But you're our best talent of the day, Daniel."

My legs were like rubber as I staggered to my feet and forced myself into a jujitsu stance, instinctively realizing that since I couldn't think clearly enough to create a peashooter, I was going to have to resort to old-fashioned hand-to-hand combat.

Unfortunately, I was still so unsteady, I think I ended up looking more like a drunk clown than a highly trained martial artist.

Number 21 was busting a gut. He mopped his sweaty brow and slung his shockwave cannon over his shoulder. "Are you guys *getting* this?" he asked the henchbeasts that were filming the shopping nightmare.

One of the crew asked, "Should we melt him too?"

"Nah," Number 21 replied. "This was just his screen test. Boss says he's still got some real important parts to play."

And then everything went black as I fell back against a tower of mac-and-cheese boxes.

Chapter 8

AS I CAME to, I could feel the henchbeasts' high-tech restraint device squeezing me from my chest down, holding me to the floor.

"Can we make a deal?" I pleaded to the two shadowy figures standing over me — and then, um, I became about as embarrassed as I've ever been in my fifteen adventure-filled Earth years.

What was holding me to the floor was not some alien-tech, carbon-fiber straitjacket, but a whole mountain of Kraft Macaroni and Cheese boxes that I'd knocked on top of myself when I passed out.

And the two figures standing above me weren't alien henchbeasts, but two twelve-year-old skate kids.

"You mean you want us to join your *crew?!*" asked the shorter chubby one.

"Dude, that's so *stoner!*" said the taller skinny one.

"Yeah, when you jumped up and the monkey dude with the big space-gun blasted you and you fell! *Whomp,* dude! Stomped like a narc! And those guys in the weird bug suits with the cameras? Totally awesome FX."

"You," I said, looking down the aisle at the brown stains on the floor that had been some of their fellow humans not long ago, "are insane."

"And you, dude, are a *magnate!* When's the show going to be on? Are you guys on YouTube?"

"You guys own both *Jackass* movies, don't you?"

"Dude. And T-shirts," he said, lifting up his buddy's sweatshirt to show an "I ♥ Jackass" decal.

I like humans; I truly do. But, sometimes it amazes me their civilization ever got off the ground.

Chapter 9

MY FRIED HEAD and body were starting to feel better as I crossed the parking lot back to my motorcycle. Pregnant women were still streaming into the store to look at the empty fish-food and motor-oil displays, but at the moment I was too bummed about losing my first battle against Number 5's crew to continue my investigation alone.

So I decided to summon Mom and Dad. I was so aching for my family right then, I even whipped up Brenda, aka Pork Chop — my annoying little sister — *out of thin air.*

"Um, Daniel, I don't think we're all going to fit," said Pork Chop, nodding at my bike.

"You are *not* still riding *motorcycles*," said Mom. "You know how I feel about them, Daniel. *Not* safe."

Dad smiled knowingly at me. It wasn't an argument worth having with Mom, although — for the record — he and I knew that unless I had an accident on my bike that involved falling into the sun or possibly a direct hit from an Opus 24/24, chances were I would escape permanent injury. And so—presto change-o—I willed some additional matter into existence and transformed my motorcycle into an awesome late-eighties vintage, wood-panel, retrofitted Dodge minivan.

"Air bags?" asked Mom.

"Side-impact air bags and ABS," I assured her and gave her the keys.

"Well, let's get going," said Dad. "Time's a wasting, and we need to convene a strategy session for dealing with Number 5 and Number 21."

The man never took a breath without having a six-point plan for it.

"And then, dear, sweet, wonderful, multitalented brother, we can all go out in the yard and polish the giant golden statue we've made of you because we love and adore you and, basically, worship your fantastic self...or *not*," said my sister, making the L-is-for-Loser sign against her forehead.

I was too tired to retaliate, so I just rolled my eyes.

"So where's home, anyway?" I asked.

"Why, right *here*," said Mom, pulling the minivan over in front of a huge Victorian house with a wraparound porch and a FOR RENT sign in the front yard.

Even without a golden statue of me in the backyard, the house was beautiful. The landlord, however, was not so easy on the eyes. We'd called the number on the sign saying we were interested in the property, and he showed up about fifteen minutes later in a gleaming, new, top-of-the-line Ferrari. Right off the bat, he was grouchy and impatient with us.

"Can we have a look around?" Dad asked.

"Let's not beat around the bush here." He'd spotted our dilapidated minivan and peered at us through his amber sunglasses. His shifty eyes darted around, sizing us up like we were so many head of cattle and he was a rancher. Or a butcher.

Chapter 10

SO, AS YOU can see, I have trust issues.

But it wouldn't have taken a ninth sense—let alone a sixth sense—to know the guy definitely wasn't cool. The next thing you know, his eyes fixed on Mom's modest engagement ring.

"Three thousand," he said, and spat some tobacco juice into the lawn.

"Dollars? *A month?!*" my mom asked.

"Plus a month's rent in advance. Security deposit. And heat and electricity are *not* included," he said, already turning back toward his luxury sports car.

"We'll take it," said Dad.

The man spun around. "Now, don't waste my time here, buddy. I have twenty properties to manage and can't waste time on deadbeats."

"Are you calling us deadbeats?" asked Mom.

Pork Chop blew a bubble and stared at him menacingly.

"All right then—a cashier's check. Six thousand dollars made payable to Ernesto Gout. And I need it today. I have a lot of other people looking at this place."

The guy tensed up a little as Dad stepped toward him, but Dad was all smiles.

"It's a deal, sir," he said, putting out his hand.

The landlord grudgingly accepted the handshake, whereupon I quickly stepped up behind him and put my hand on the back of his head, causing him to go rigid like somebody had dropped an ice cube down his shirt.

Cool Alien Hunter power number 141: Telepathic Attitude Adjustments.

"So, would cash be okay?" I asked.

"Yes, yes, of course. Cash would be fine," he said, quickly coming around.

"And how about if *you* bring it *to us* by, oh, say, noon."

For a moment it looked like he was going to lose his lunch, but he nodded.

"And we'll need you to call the electric and gas companies and arrange to pay that yourself, okay?"

"Yeah-yeah, sure-sure."

"And, here, why don't we trade cars? You take the minivan, so you can have some more room for stuff when you run our errands. And we'll keep the Ferrari."

"Great idea."

"All right then. If you can just give me the keys to the

house and your car, I'll let you go to the bank and get us our money."

"Yes, sir," he said.

It all goes to show that you can't always believe first impressions.

Or, if you don't like your first impression, then change it. I mean, if you're an Alien Hunter.

Chapter 11

AFTER MR. GOUT returned with the money, we sent him off to get some lumber and other things to help alienproof the house. His attitude was much improved—he actually seemed happy about it.

"Your abilities are getting sharper," remarked Dad, "but you're going to need a bit more than that for Number 5. In fact, I've managed to update his profile, and I created a brief dossier I want you to digest before dinner."

"And you aren't going out till you've taken a shower and done your laundry," added Mom. "You look like a raga-muffin. And tomorrow you're getting a haircut."

I guess it's a little weird that I let myself get bossed around by people that are essentially products of my imagination; but what kind of parents would they be otherwise?

"Sure, Mom," I humored her. Meantime, I went to check out some updates and relevant List computer information that Dad had helped me locate on Number 5 and Number 21.

You don't make it into The List's top ten without a pretty terrifying résumé to back it up, but the more I found out about Number 5, the more it was clear this was going to be my biggest test yet.

Like the electric eels on Earth, his species had evolved in murky swamp waters where electrical powers gave a creature a distinct advantage. Only, of course, his species had evolved a little more than any eel. Not only were Number 5 and his kin able to sense and stun with electricity, but they could also manipulate the electrical impulses in their prey's brains and actually hypnotize them into doing whatever they wanted.

According to recent reports, it wasn't uncommon to find Number 5's species living with a handful of attending servants, who would do everything from cleaning to cooking *themselves* for dinner.

In the field of electromagnetics, Number 5 was described as something of an artist—you know, like in the way Genghis Khan was an artist with battlefield tactics and ruthless leadership. Oh, sorry…maybe you missed that part of world history class.

Also, he was a dynamo of energy. Literally. Where an electric eel could generate a few kilowatts—enough to kill the population of, say, a bathtub—Number 5 could generate enough electricity to fry an entire water park full of people...and even those out in the parking lot.

As to Number 21, the space ape that had gotten the jump on me in S-Mart, I discovered his show-biz name was Dougie Starshine and that he'd been credited as the production assistant and casting director on Number 5's last dozen shows—and that he was no weakling, either.

That alien miscreant was wanted for murder in a half dozen galaxies, and it looked like he had some pretty serious psychic warfare talents. I mean, maybe a twenty-one ranking doesn't quite compare to a top-ten baddie, but if you're the type of reader who likes a little perspective, consider that Joe and I had figured out that if Superman were evil *and* real (in fact, he is loosely based on a real alien from the Crab Nebula), he'd come in at about number thirty-seven.

Real aliens seldom have weaknesses as obvious as kryptonite.

Chapter 12

DAD AND I went out back and did some jujitsu training—and savate, tae kwon do, taekkyon, aikido, judo, and
glima for good measure—and held a brief tactical planning session afterward.

He'd decided that when you boiled it right down, all
that Number 21 had done to me was seize the advantage
by using the element of surprise.

If there is a kryptonite for me, then there you have it:
because my powers are directly linked to my imagination,
I have to be thinking clearly in order to make the best use
of them.

By hitting me with that concussion-inducing shockwave, Number 21 had been able to keep me disoriented
and unable, for instance, to visualize any weapons—or
summon my alien-butt-kicking friends.

"Hey, Mom," I yelled. She was sitting on the back porch reading a book, *The Elephant-Keeper's Secret Kite,* that I'd picked up for her. Have I mentioned that I love elephants and that it's a little-known fact that they originated on my home planet?

"What's for dinner?" I asked.

"I have no idea," she replied. "All we have here is a tin of caviar I found in the mailbox along with a lot of other old junk mail."

"Caviar?" I asked. "As in fish eggs?"

"A lot of people consider it a delicacy, Daniel," she reminded me, holding out the package. It was still in its clear plastic mailer, addressed to "Female Resident."

I tore open the bag and read the note that came with the can:

A gift to the women of Holliswood from the KHAW news team, in gratitude for your kindness to visiting film producers. Bon appétit!

Caviar from the local news station? Well go ahead and chalk up mystery number 112 for me to solve already. And, while you're at the board, why don't you put me down for what is really only my second bad pun ever — although in this case I think you'll agree it's completely unavoidable — because there was something *very fishy* going on in this town.

Chapter 13

SINCE I REALLY did not want caviar for dinner—or ever—I sent Mr. Gout out for some KFC original recipe. I knew my friends, especially Joe, would never forgive me if I didn't summon them for the Colonel Sanders gorge fest. Joe nearly cried with happiness when he saw Mr. Gout come in the door with the big red-and-white buckets.

Then Dana, Willy, Joe, and Emma and I said good night to my parents and hopped into the Ferrari. The only problem was the five of us couldn't fit in a two-seater sports car.

"Leave Dana here," said Joe.

"No way," said Dana, "You're the one who smells like Colonel Sanders's gym shorts."

"I'll stay behind if you guys want," said the ever-sacrificing Emma. "Even though all *I* smell like is *coleslaw* because nobody ever asks what *I* want to eat for dinner."

Emma always serves us a generous helping of grief for eating meat.

"Hey, you kids," said Dad, who was standing on the front lawn, laughing at us along with Pork Chop. "Take the minivan," he suggested. "I made some modifications that will help quite a bit with your, um, errands tonight."

Willy had already clambered out of the overstuffed Ferrari and was sliding open the minivan's side-panel door.

"*Dudes.* You gotta come check this out!"

Chapter 14

DAD HAD CONVERTED the minivan into a cross between Scooby Doo's Mystery Machine and a NASA command center.

The spacious, now shag-carpeted interior was blinking, pulsing, and humming with sensor displays, joysticks, trackballs, touchpads, data visors, relay panels, heads-up displays, sampling hoods, and holographic imagers.

"This is great, Dad," I said. "So how's everything work?"

"I'm sure a genius like you can figure it out in no time," said Pork Chop, snapping her bubblegum.

"It's all very user-friendly," said Dad. "I don't think any of you will have any trouble getting the hang of it."

"Actually, it's my four copilots who'll be getting the hang of it," I said. "I'm driving."

They groaned but settled into the back of the van without another note of complaint as I drove toward the outskirts of town. They're good friends like that.

As we made our way down the quaint residential streets, you couldn't help noticing the windows of nearly every house glowing with the eerie blue flicker of TV and computer screens. This thing called Contemporary America—and its obsession with televisions, game systems, and computers—has gone a little far if you ask me. Some call it the Information Age, but I'd tend to say it's more the Sitting-on-one's-butt-and-letting-other-people-do-the-thinking-for-you Age.

"You guys find anything useful back there?" I asked, turning onto Mulberry from Larch.

"Yes, I think I have our first target!" said Joe. "There's a whole mess of 'em in a building about a half mile from us. Hang a left here and then a right at the next stoplight."

"How many are there?" asked Willy, practicing some jujitsu moves in the middle of the van.

"Can't tell yet. Hang on, okay?" Joe remained intent on his data feed. I turned at the light onto a commercial street lined with stores and shopping plazas.

"Okay, it's up there on the right," said Joe. "Should say 'White Castle' on it...and it's absolutely infested with...*hamburgers!*"

We pelted him with food wrappers, empty soda cans, a couple of dirty sneakers. I should've remembered that *no* mission is more important to Joe than filling his supersize-me stomach.

Chapter 15

JOE PRACTICALLY HAD to be held down to be kept from leaping out of the van as we passed the White Castle.

I steered back to our original route, but we didn't get very far. A man, covered from head to toe in mud, staggered out of the bushes and into the middle of the road.

I swerved and hit the brakes.

"Hey," I yelled out the window. "You need some help?"

He ignored me and staggered up the lawn of a house whose windows—like all the others we'd seen—were flickering blue from TV and computer displays.

"Yo," yelled Willy, climbing out of the van after him. "You okay?"

The man must have heard him—unless he was deaf or had mud in his ears—but he just walked up to the house and right smack into the closed front door. After a minute or two, the door opened, and we caught a glimpse of a pregnant woman as he pushed his way through and disappeared inside.

"Rough day at work, I guess," said Dana.

"Maybe he's an alligator wrestler," suggested Joe.

"Alligators don't live this far north, stupid," said Emma. "But clearly he was coming from someplace muddy."

"The closest body of water is two point one miles south-southeast of here," said Dana, clicking away on a computer in the back of the minivan. "That roughly lines up with the direction he was coming from."

"Step on it, driver!" said Willy.

"Hey, I'm in charge around here," I said and added, "as should be obvious to a bunch of people who depend on my imagination for their very existence."

"Sorry, your highness," said Joe, returning the flurry of food wrappers, soda cans, and sneakers that had nailed him earlier.

We'd just turned onto County Road 23 when Emma suddenly shrieked like a banshee.

A dog had run into the street just feet away from our car.

Chapter 16

I BRAKED SO hard that everybody in the backseats ended up in the front seats.

"What's with all the jaywalking delays?" I grumbled. I had an investigation to conduct here.

"Aw," said Emma, sitting up and looking at the poor animal shivering in the van's headlights.

"Somebody tried to *burn* him," she exclaimed as we got out of the van. She gathered the medium-sized brown dog in her arms.

"Are you sure you want to pick him up like that?" asked Joe. "He's, like, really muddy."

Emma shot him a reproachful glance.

"Judging from the shape of the burn marks," said Willy, petting the dog's head, "I'd say an alien firearm did this.

He's a lucky pup to have escaped with only some singed fur."

"He doesn't have a collar," Dana observed.

"Which is just one more reason why we're taking him with us," said Emma. "We'll check with the animal shelter to see if anybody's missing a dog, and, if not, we'll adopt him. And, for now, his name will be Lucky, just like Willy said."

I thought about this for a moment. Unlike the rest of them, Lucky wouldn't just disappear when I needed to be alone. So if Emma adopted him and then Emma wasn't around for a bit, the dog would be *my* responsibility. I felt like a parent having an awkward moment at PetSmart.

"Um, I think we better leave him here. I mean, he was probably going someplace—" I broke off. Emma looked like she was deciding exactly how to conduct my public execution.

"Right," I said. "Bring him into the van already." I'd figure this out later. He *was* a pretty sweet-looking dog, at least under the burned fur and inch-thick mud.

Hey, I may be an alien, but I still have a heart.

Chapter 17

WE TRAVELED ABOUT a quarter mile down an un-painted, heavily potholed strip of asphalt that saw more traffic from combines and livestock trailers than passenger vehicles. I knew we'd hit the boondocks when we saw something far stranger than a farm animal emerge about twenty feet in front of the van.

It was an alien picnic. Right there in the middle of the road was a cluster of Number 5's henchbeasts.

"Um…" wondered Joe. "Why aren't they attacking us?"

"It worked!" said Dana. "See, I put us in *stealth* mode. We can see them, but they *can't* see us. Or hear us, for that matter. A mile or so back I turned on a cloaking device that renders the van invisible."

"Go ahead," she continued, "test it out. Drive up closer."

As we slowly approached, we could see some of them were munching on chicken wings. Not buffalo- or BBQ-style, though…they were the kind with feathers still on them and blood still in them. They guzzled cans of *motor* oil to wash them down and tossed the empties to the ground and stomped on them like they were at a fraternity party.

And then we noticed one henchbeast had something that looked suspiciously like a cat's tail hanging out of its mouth.

"That's *so* disgusting," said Joe. "I mean people say they could eat a horse when they're hungry, but that's just an expression. What kind of monster would actually eat a poor little kitty?"

"Stay here, Lucky," said Emma, and before the rest of us could stop her, she'd jumped out of the van and was sprinting toward the aliens.

Chapter 18

I'VE GOT TO hand it to Emma—for a peacenik, she really knows how to lay down some hurt. That first alien she decked must have thought it had been teleported back up into space for all the stars and blackness it was suddenly seeing.

Still, this was a case of seven versus one, and, though she managed to knock down a henchbeast and had delivered some serious facial rearrangement to another, she was soon at the uncomfortable center of an alien pileup.

Willy was the first to reach her side. He grabbed the nearest henchbeast and threw him a dozen yards straight into a tree. The young maple shook and dropped a lot of sticks and leaves but fared better than the alien—which shook and dropped most of its legs.

Joe, Emma, and I managed to take out another two, but the other aliens had remembered their guns by this point and were laying down some heavy fire that kept us playing far more defense than offense.

That is, until it occurred to me that I could turn their high-powered plasma guns into Super Soakers.

Willy was quick to notice the change, and he jumped forward, taking a shot right in the chest.

"Oh no!" he screamed, "I'm *me-eh-eh-elting!!!*" And then he collapsed to the ground.

"Or...*not!*" he said, leaping back up and adopting an intimidating martial arts stance.

Alien henchbeasts tend not to be as deep or as sensitive as human beings, but they do have faces, so it's pretty easy to tell what emotions they're feeling. In this case, the look on their ugly mugs is what you could safely call *terror*.

For a few seconds, they continued to halfheartedly squirt lame streams of water at Willy and my friends...and then dropped their plastic toys and scattered into the woods.

"You okay, Emma?" asked Dana, as our friend got back to her feet.

"It *was* a cat," she said, pointing to a pile of torn flea collars on the pavement.

We nodded sympathetically. I spotted a satchel one of the aliens had been carrying and began to rummage through it.

"Promise me, Daniel," said Emma. "We're going to get every last one of these monsters."

"That's job one," I reassured her. But I was preoccupied with something I'd found in the satchel. Something very strange, and distressing.

Chapter 19

IT WAS A small piece of jewelry from my home planet.

My people are incredible and distinctive craftsmen, and I instantly identified the small silver pendant of an elephant as genuine Alparian handiwork, not some dimestore knockoff.

In fact, elephant pendants like this were commonly worn by adults who leave the planet, emblems of homeworld solidarity. My mother and father had both received them when they had graduated from the Academy and accepted jobs in the Protectorship. As far as I knew, they'd never taken them off.

So what on earth—or any other planet, for that matter—were a bunch of Number 5's henchbeasts doing walking around with an Alpar Nokian elephant necklace?

It had to be one of my first memories, that little silver

elephant hanging from my mother's neck. I'd play with it endlessly, watching it twirl and catch the light whenever she held me in her arms...though I hadn't thought about it in years.

I wiped away some moisture from my eye before it technically became a tear. *One more mystery for me to solve*, I thought with a sigh, putting the pendant in my pocket.

Just then I had this really weird sensation that I was being watched, and I spun around. But there was nothing—just cricket-infested woods.

"Joe," I yelled into the van, "are you picking up any alien life-forms on the scanners?"

"Nothing but regular wildlife. Those cat eaters we scared off are miles away by now."

Great, I thought. *Now Number 5's made me paranoid, on top of everything else.*

Chapter 20

AFTER A MILE or so, the county road crossed over the freeway, and we pulled into a small Exxon minimart at the end of the off-ramp to regroup about where the night's mission was headed. We got some waters and sodas, and Joe bought a couple dozen bags of chips, a fistful of jerky sticks, and at least a dozen Hostess bakery products.

That was normal, but here's the weird part: Joe actually stopped eating in the back of the van *before* he'd finished inhaling his third bag of nacho cheese chips. Even weirder, he paused to place a crumb inside what looked like a miniature microwave oven.

"Fifty-three percent Benton, Iowa; thirty-two percent Edison, New Jersey; eleven percent Las Piedras, Mexico; three percent Ankang, China. And trace quantities from, oh, a planet that's about twenty-five thousand light years away from Earth."

"*What* are you talking about?" asked Dana.

"That corn chip. This machine can pinpoint the origins of any sample you put inside it. In this case, a corn chip."

"Your corn chip has extraterrestrial ingredients?" asked Dana, wrinkling her cute little nose.

"Well, it's mostly from Iowa—probably the corn part," said Joe.

"It's no surprise, really," I said. "The List tells us there are *how* many thousand aliens living here on Earth?"

"Probably one of them works at the snack factory and sneezed on the production line," said Dana.

"Yeah," said Emma, "or they're trying to poison the population or something."

"It's possible," said Joe, sticking another handful of chips in his mouth. "Aw I cun...sayfersher is...day...tayse...perrygood."

"Think you can fit some caviar in there?" I asked, handing Joe a can from my backpack. It was the tin that mom had found in the mailbox.

He put the whole can inside and slammed the door shut. The machine hummed while Joe swallowed the last of the chips.

"Yeah, this one's not going to earn 'organic' certification, either. The paper looks like it might have come from Oregon trees, but the metal and stuff inside is definitely from a galaxy far, far away."

"Let me guess," I said, "Number 5's home planet."

"On the button," said Joe.

"Guys," said Dana, hunkering over her console. "I'm seeing signs of alien activity a few hundred yards from here. And there's some sort of freaky transmission coming from a TV relay station just up that hill over there."

Against the starry sky, we could see a sinister red light blinking atop a steel-framed communications tower.

"Listen to this."

The minivan's speaker system began to play a decidedly unearthly series of clicks, moans, and static.

Lucky bared his teeth and made a low growl.

"Atta boy," said Emma, stroking his neck reassuringly. "Let's go rid Earth of some aliens."

Chapter 21

THE RELAY STATION'S access road was barricaded by a chain-link gate.

"Want me to make it go away?" asked Willy, already aiming his plasma cannon at it.

"It's easier to spy on aliens when they don't hear you coming," I said.

So we left Lucky to guard the van, and, as stealthily as an Alien Hunter and his four imagined friends can manage, we jumped the fence. It was fifteen feet high, but we can do tall buildings in a single bound, so it really wasn't an issue.

We snuck up the hardscrabble road on foot. At the top of the hill and inside another fence—this one topped with concertina wire—we found a pretty typical broadcast substation: a small forest of towers, satellite dishes, antennas, and transformers. The small control shack also looked to have been built by human hands.

Everything, in fact, seemed pretty normal—except that the door to the shack had been blown off its hinges, and there was an eerie blue glow emanating from within...and, of course, the air was filled with the disgusting stink of aliens.

We broke out some night-vision binoculars and long-range microphones and crept closer. There were a half dozen henchbeasts inside the shack, guzzling motor oil and laughing their ugly butts off as one of them edited video footage.

The transmissions were surreal scenes of townspeople doing dances, singing a capella, and, always at the end, getting vaporized. That especially sent the aliens into hysterics.

Next they uploaded a scene of pregnant women converging on a country farmhouse.

"That Number 5's a stallion," said one of them, guffawing conspiratorially.

"Yeah, especially for a fish," replied another, causing the rest to roll on the floor with laughter.

Just then the picture on the monitors changed to the glowering image of their boss, and they quickly stood at nervous attention.

"Are you no-talent alien clowns having a good time?" asked Number 5.

"Yes, sir!—I mean no, sir!—We mean—"

"Spare me the stupidity," said Number 5. "And see if you can't spare yourselves and me yet *another* production delay. Our friend the Alien Hunter is forty-five meters away, and he's armed to the teeth."

"Well, so much for the element of surprise," said Joe.

Willy cracked his knuckles and then, in his best Bruce Willis impersonation, said, "Lock and load."

We didn't like using guns ourselves, but I had to agree with the sentiment.

Chapter 22

NOTE TO SELF: when fighting hand-to-hand with rubber-skeletoned aliens—which some of these evidently were—remember that thing Sir Isaac Newton said about every action being met with an equal and opposite *re*action.

Because no sooner had I landed a devastating round-house kick to the head of one of the henchbeasts than I was sailing through the night like I'd just jumped off a ten-story building onto a trampoline.

I somehow managed to land on my feet on the far side of the control shack and was ready to spring back into action, but my friends had already figured out how to deal with these overly flexible aliens. You simply tie one of their limbs to a fixed object, such as the steel girders of the broadcast tower, and then you run with their bodies in the opposite direction.

Then, when you can't run any farther, you let go and — *bang!* — the creatures snap back into themselves with such force that they explode like dropped water balloons. Only they're filled with some sort of sticky greenish syrup rather than water.

Gross but effective.

The other type of henchbeast we encountered wasn't quite so stretchy but had its own surprise — some sort of gland on the abdomen that could spray a jet of foul black acid more than thirty feet.

We found they weren't very good at aiming up, however. The secret was to jump into the air and then crush them from above — *splat!* — just like a foot squashing a bug.

But since they each weighed about a hundred fifty pounds, they left your sneakers a whole lot messier.

Chapter 23

ONCE WE'D SAFELY dispatched the last of them, we ducked into the control shack, hoping to find some clues. It was worrisome that Number 5 often seemed to know my whereabouts.

There was no sign of him, however.

"So what were they up to in here?" asked Joe.

"I think Number 5's getting ready for a new show," I said. "Our friends were probably uploading the footage to an extraterrestrial receiver for postproduction. Joe, can you figure out anything useful about this setup?"

He was already poring over the equipment, following wires and examining switches and displays.

"Yeah, it looks like most of the data is getting broadcast straight up into space. There's a small signal coming back, though. Probably a guidance beacon, but it might be something else. Here, let me see if I can get it on this set here."

He moved some wires to different jacks and threw a couple of switches. And then we saw what might have been the most sickening thing I'd ever seen.

And, yes, I've been on the Internet before.

Chapter 24

IMAGINE THE THEATER for *American Idol* during the season finale. Now make it bigger—like Madison Square Garden in New York or the Staples Center in Los Angeles. And now quadruple its seating capacity. And now replace the mostly polite, family-oriented audience of American Idol with the loud, obnoxious fans of, say, Jerry Springer or Howard Stern. And have them not be human.

Have some be three headed; have some be lobster clawed; have some wearing space suits; have some glowing with orange radiation; have some be nothing more than dense clouds of blue vapor; have some that look like huge unblinking eyeballs on mushroom stalks; have some with hammer heads, some with needle noses, some with feathers, some with frog legs, some with turtle backs, and some that look like Chinese dumplings with sea-urchin spines and metal helmets...well, that at least starts to paint the scene.

But that wasn't the sickening part.

What made us gasp in horror was the stage, where the scenes we'd watched on the monitor were now being played for the alien horde's viewing pleasure.

A father and his daughter getting terrified by a microphone-wielding Number 5...and then liquefied by blaster rays.

A family—and even their dog—dancing to seventies disco hits...and then melted by blaster rays.

A TV news anchor break dancing on her desk...and then, in a flash of light, getting transformed into a steaming pool of swampy liquid.

And then *me,* getting knocked senseless by Number 21 in S-Mart.

The audience loved every second of it. Even through all of the bits of static and fuzz, you could see the jeers, the sneers, the laughter, the pumping fists, claws, and tentacles of those assembled interplanetary creeps.

Then, I heard Number 5's voice boom through the arena. "And that, my fellow producers, is just the trailer for the hottest new entertainment phenomenon we're calling *endertainment.* Watch the skies for more episodes—and a *sizzling* premiere that'll leave you *dying* for more."

Without saying a word, the five of us started smashing everything in the shack.

Sparks flew, and the air filled with the scent of shorted fuses and ozone as we hurled mixing boards, editing decks, holoform display units, and a bunch of other things we didn't bother to identify before we trashed them.

And then, as I reached to pull one of the monitors off its wall-mounted bracket, Number 5's image flickered to life on the screen.

"I thought you were the Alien *Hunter,* not the Alien *Vandal,*" he laughed.

I was speechless. How did he do that TV trick? It looked like a regular old set.

"You'll be happy to know the broadcast was completed before you destroyed any of this equipment."

"I don't care," I managed to say.

"Don't you?" he said. "I'm not sure I believe you. Not that I suppose it matters. The only thing that would be a help is if you stuck around town till we're ready for the final episode. You have a starring role in it, you know."

"You're not even going to make it to episode two, you fishy freak."

"Ah-ah-ah-ah!" he laughed at me. "Very good, young Alien Hunter. That's just the kind of bravado the audience loves to see. And it will make it all the funnier when I *kill you in a live broadcast.*"

Chapter 25

"DUDE," SAID JOE as I hurled the monitor through the window. "He's totally toying with you."

"Let him keep thinking that," I said—although, truth be told, I was getting pretty freaked at this point.

"How can he possibly keep seeing me through TV screens like that, Joe?"

"Maybe he's got them reverse-wired somehow, has them working as cameras."

"Is that possible?"

"Almost anything's possible if you have alien technology on your side."

"Can you take a look and find out for us?"

"Sure," said Joe. "Of course, it would've been easier if you hadn't thrown it out the window and smashed it into a thousand pieces...but I'll see what I can do."

He stepped out of the shack to gather up the remains.

"Okay," I said to the rest of them. "You guys have any big ideas here? Personally, I'm starting to wonder if going after Number 5 wasn't a big mistake."

"But he'll keep killing animals if you don't stop him," said Emma.

"And humans," said Willy.

"And probably you," said Dana.

"You guys are a great help," I said.

Chapter 26

JOE DIDN'T FIND anything strange in the wrecked TV. No nanocameras, no light-sensitive data films, no reverse-broadcast microtransceivers. Which left me one conclusion—Number 5's electromagnetic powers were greater than I'd even begun to imagine.

I mean, the only thing I could figure was that he was actually able to *inhabit* electronic devices. And, in a world as wired as this one was becoming...well, there wasn't much to keep this soulless creep from turning the entire human race into an unpaid variety show and then committing the worst extinction event the planet had ever seen.

Just to be safe, I had the gang run a complete analysis on the van's equipment, and, when we made it back to the house, we shut off the main circuit breaker in the basement and cut the phone lines.

Clearly, if I was going to find a way to surprise Number 5—and I'd been miserably failing at it so far—I couldn't have him watching me through the electrical sockets.

I turned to my family and friends. "If you were Number 5, what would be the last thing you'd expect of a young Alien Hunter bent on wiping your foul-smelling stain off the face of the planet?"

"Acting normal for once in your life?" offered Pork Chop.

I was about to give her the L-is-for-Loser sign, but that's when it hit me. Tomorrow morning I was going to do exactly what any *normal* kid my age would do. I'd get up, get dressed, drink some orange juice, eat a frosted strawberry Pop-Tart, and go to high school.

Number 5 wouldn't expect *that* in a million years.

Chapter 27

DANA AND I had English class first period, although maybe *class* isn't quite the right word for it. It was more like a *holding pen* in which the substitute teacher and the students had collectively agreed to spend fifty-five minutes doing as little productive activity as was humanly possible.

The sub clearly just wanted to keep things quiet enough to avoid the attention of any hallway-roving administrators. And the kids, for their part, were taking full advantage of the situation. Some were texting friends; some were chatting idly; some were staring off into space; and two boys were actually sleeping at their desks. The closest thing to learning taking place in the room was a single dark-haired girl reading some manga.

"And, in this great country's quest to create a democratic, self-governing citizenry," Dana declaimed to whomever was listening — namely, me — "it was determined that the most important function of its free and public schools was to help its children become motivated, engaged, and eager-to-learn participants in the democratic process; that although the downward-sloping road to lowest-common denominators might have seemed the easiest to travel, the job of teachers, parents, and the larger community was to provide an education that showcased the highway to mathematics, reading, writing, problem solving, and critical thinking as the more compelling and rewarding route."

"You are *so* weird," I told her.

"Aren't you always reminding me that I'm a product of *your* imagination?"

"You have a point there."

"You mean about the failures of this country's educational system or that stuff about how if I'm weird, you have only yourself to blame?"

"Both, really," I said.

It was frustrating to see these kids wasting this opportunity. I know I'm not the oldest or wisest entity in the cosmos, but life is short no matter what planet you're from — way too short to waste chances to learn.

Plus — as has been proved only a couple million times — List aliens have a much better time taking advantage of *undereducated* people than *well-educated* ones. Trust me, in my alien world, the ranks of abductees, hosts, slaves, and murder victims include a lot more TV and video-game addicts than they do book readers.

I saw a group of girls gather around an iPhone to watch a little red-carpet footage from some second-rate award show.

And then I had an idea.

Because this was *supposed* to be an English class, I decided to make up for some of the time they'd lost and uploaded into every student's brain a couple of my favorite human books—which I've of course memorized word-for-word in both text and audio formats—*The Catcher in the Rye* and *Stranger in a Strange Land*. And then, as a bonus, I gave them the entire contents of Wikipedia.

The poor sub must have thought he was getting punked. All the kids—having suddenly discovered the joy of a good book for the first time—were lining up and asking him for more things to read.

It felt good to put things somewhat back on track here, but I sensed there was a lot more fixing to do in this school, so Dana and I gathered up our books and went out into the hallway.

Chapter 28

ONE OF THE many cool things about Robert A. Heinlein's classic *Stranger in a Strange Land,* which is about a guy with alien superpowers living among humans here on Earth, is this thing called "grokking." *Grok* is a Martian word that literally means "to drink," but it's one of those words—in both the book and real life—that often means a whole lot more. When you grok something, you're saying you *get it*.

Like when Dana and I stepped into the linoleum-floored corridor, I instantly grokked the fear, confusion, and hopelessness of about a hundred freshman filing, zombie-like, down the hall toward the back of the building.

"Number 5," I whispered, and Dana nodded in agreement. I quickly made us look a little younger—I'd make an excellent plastic surgeon if I were into that kind of stuff—and we joined the end of the line.

"Where are we going?" I asked the little messy-haired kid in front of me.

"We've got another practice for the big musical, stupid," he replied.

"Ah, the big musical," said Dana. "When's that happening again?"

"Saturday, you moron. What are you guys, foreign-exchange students?"

"Something like that," I said, putting my hand on his neck and quickly erasing his memory of this conversation, just in case.

We exited the building and came to a silent stop on the sidewalk next to the school parking lot where, a moment later, two yellow buses, each driven by a hench-beast, screeched to a halt.

The kids wordlessly broke into two groups and climbed aboard.

"You want to do something about this?" Dana asked me.

"Not yet," I said. "Sounds like this is another rehearsal, so I'm pretty sure they're not in immediate peril. Number 5's too much of a perfectionist to kill prematurely. He's going to want the best, biggest bang he can get on Saturday."

We broke away from the group and hid behind the rear bus. Dana slapped a small magnetic device under the bumper.

"Homing beacon," she said, as the bus doors closed and the buses squealed away from the curb, "so we can track where they're taking them for the practice session and hopefully see where Number 5's intending to film Holliswood's grand finale this weekend."

We returned to the building, and I noticed two pregnant teachers standing silently in the courtyard, staring up at the sky. I'd never seen so many pregnant women in one town. Time to get to the bottom of this.

"How long have you been pregnant?" I asked the closer one.

"Four weeks," she replied.

"Four weeks?" said Dana, her eyes nearly bugging out of her head. "You're a little big for four weeks, don't you think? Aren't you worried?"

"No, I'm just *happy*," she said like a very, very bad actress reading a very, very lame script.

Then I did something I don't normally like to do because it makes me feel queasy on the best of days. I used my X-ray vision... and looked inside her belly.

I'd describe to you in detail what I saw, except you'd never forgive me if I did.

Chapter 29

"ALIEN SPAWN," I explained to Dana as diplomatically as I could. "Number 5's, by the look of them."

"Nasty," said Dana. "So all these pregnant women in town are actually filled with little Number 5s?"

"That's my theory," I said.

"That's *horrible!*" said Dana, gasping.

"And I'm guessing the 'caviar' mailing from the television station is how it happened."

"Which means the station is probably one of the first, if not *the* first, place Number 5 attacked. Let's go have a look!"

"You may be right, Dana, but I want to check out a few things before going over there."

"Like what? Gym class?"

"No. I have to go see somebody."

"Who?"

"Never mind. I'll see you back at the house, okay?"

"*Who* are you going to see, Daniel?" she asked, tapping her foot impatiently.

"Well…" I started to explain, but then I clapped her out of existence. It was an awkward thing to explain to anybody, let alone Dana.

Chapter 30

I PULLED THE van into the diner lot and spotted Judy Blue Eyes through the plate-glass window, shuttling a brown-rimmed coffee pot back and forth to customers along the counter.

I made my way inside, pulled my "Relax" cap down over my eyes, and took a stool across from the rotating pie display.

She had recovered well from the other night, and it would be an understatement to say she was looking pretty cute.

"Hey, you!" she said, spotting me and causing my alien heart to flop around in my chest like a fish in the bottom of a rowboat.

"Hey, J-J-," I started to say but, fortunately, she cut off my nervous stutter with a glass of water and a menu.

"So, um, how's it going?" I finally managed to ask.

"Good. How's it going with *you?*" she asked.

"Good."

"Want another of those grilled cheese sandwiches you liked so much—with a slice of pickle in it?"

"Sure. Great. Thanks." I was doing well with the one-word sentences. "Look, um, Judy—"

"Yes?" she asked, batting her eyes and causing me to forget what I had meant to ask her.

"So, has anything…unusual happened since the other night?"

"Unusual? Like what?"

"Like, um, anything weird?"

"Where? Here, at the diner?"

"Yeah, or in your neighborhood, or at school."

"*My* school is always weird—my parents have been homeschooling me since eighth grade. It totally stinks."

"I'm sure they're doing what's best for you."

"Yeah, completely destroying my social life is just what the doctor ordered."

"Seriously, you never go to school?"

"Pretty much just for standardized tests. Like twice a year."

"So when do you get out to see your friends?"

"Friends? I'm lucky to get out for piano lessons. I took this job pretty much just so I could talk to other human beings." *How ironic that she had found herself talking to a nonhuman instead*, I thought. "Only problem is it's usually old truckers, municipal employees, and police. My parents

88

figure it's good experience for me and a chance for me to earn some money for college."

"I'm impressed."

"Yeah, they seem to think I'll get into a better school this way. And who knows? Maybe they're right. Maybe Mulberry Avenue Academy *is* better than Holliswood High."

"What's Mulberry Avenue Academy?"

"Mulberry Avenue is the street my house is on. I was trying to make a joke, stu."

"Stu? Um, my name's Daniel."

"Stu's not just short for Stuart, *stu*pid."

I was unprepared for that, but I was pretty sure she was flirting.

"So you feel like it's a good idea to tease me even with a name like you've got?" I said pointing at her name tag. "I mean, it seems to me if you want to go that way—"

"My real last name's McGillicutty. My boss couldn't spell it over the phone to the uniform supplier, so he put the order through as Judy Blue Eyes."

"McGillicutty, huh?" I was tempted to tell her name sounded just like a substance, magillakedi, that's excreted by a three-hundred-pound centipede-like creature from Frizia Nine and is one of the three worst-smelling compounds ever discovered . . . but then I thought better of it.

"So, remind me. . . . Did you say you wanted that sandwich, stu?"

We were staring pretty hard into each other's eyes at this point, and I was feeling a little giddy. "Sure, a sandwich would be great."

Chapter 31

ONE MINUTE JUDY was herself—smiling, bouncing down the length of the counter to pass my order through the kitchen window—and the next minute, the diner was almost as surreal as an alien picnic.

All at once the volume on the TV set above the cash register went from mute to ear busting. A number from that *High School Musical* show started to crescendo, and suddenly Judy was juggling coleslaw cups and then twirling the two-foot-long pepper mill like she was a majorette.

Then the volume went back down, and, without missing a beat, she was back leaning across the counter looking at me.

"That's funny," she said, putting down the mill. "You asked for pepper, right?"

"Um, yeah, sure. Listen," I said, getting out my wallet.

"I just remembered I have to walk the dog." Even weirder than Judy's juggling routine was the fact that Zac Efron from *High School Musical* was starting to look a little like Number 5 to me. Sure sign it was time to split.

"Oh, okay," she said, looking a little surprised.

"Just promise me you'll keep your eyes open for anything strange, okay?"

"You betcha, cutie."

Did I mention Alien Hunter superability number 415? Yeah, I can blush so hard that Santa could probably give Rudolph a season off and have *me* guide his sleigh at night.

So my big giant red head and I stuttered "Th-th-thanks," and left a nice tip on the counter.

I scanned the room for danger on my way out and noticed a few shady dudes in one of the corner booths. Their overcoat collars were turned up, their rain hats pulled down, and, though they were taking pains to hide their faces behind their menus, I got a definite glimpse of *blue skin.*

I quickly looked away, continued on as if nothing was wrong, and, as I passed the coffee machine, grabbed two full pots and threw the boiling-hot liquid right into their laps.

I knew it wasn't going to do any real damage, but there's nothing like a good old-fashioned, lawsuit-worthy, scorching-hot coffee spill to really tick someone off.

It worked like a charm.

Chapter 32

I WAS OUT the door and into the parking lot in a flash, four coffee-scalded aliens hot on my tail.

"I hate when that happens," I said pointing at the damp, yellow stains on their poorly fitting pants. "*So-o* embarrassing!"

"You. Are. So. *Dead*," said the biggest one. He pressed a button on a small electronic device he was holding, and the back door on a tractor-trailer parked at the rear of the lot rolled open, revealing an interstellar transport container. That could only mean one thing: something very big, very bad, and very *foreign* was about to appear on the scene.

An unnerving roar emanated from within, and, a moment later, an enormous space creature leaped out into the parking lot.

With the body of a six-hundred-pound lion, a giant

ant's head with wicked-sharp mouthparts, and a stinger on its tail the size of a baseball bat, the creature gave the impression that it wasn't here to march in the annual firemen's parade.

It let out another roar and pawed at the pavement like an angry bull, its antennae pointing at me like twin rifle barrels.

"Um, why's it looking at *me*?" I asked the aliens. One of them responded with a grizzly voice.

"Every day since it was a kitten, its trainers have punished it with a stick that was coated in the scent of your pathetic Alparian species. It may have never met you personally, but, trust us, it *hates your guts*."

"Um," I said, trying to decide whether giant lions or giant ants scared me more, "you wouldn't have any spare deodorant I could borrow, would you?"

The henchbeasts thought that was hilarious.

Chapter 33

I DON'T KNOW if you're a fan of nature documentaries or otherwise familiar with the African savanna's ecosystem, but the truth is that even if the lion is King of the Jungle, he's not quite an all-powerful ruler.

The only truly supreme creature on that continent—the one creature that *no* other animal will go against—is the African elephant.

Weighing in at seven tons, more than twenty times the size of the largest lion, five times the size of a rhino, and with ivory-hardened tusks capable of tearing open a Jeep, there isn't much that's going to risk challenging the will of a full-grown bull elephant.

So I changed myself into one.

Although, in deference to my adversary's mutant alien

status, I included some special bonus features that I'll explain shortly.

Unfortunately, my sudden shape change didn't have the immediate effect I intended. Instead of leaping back into his cage, scared out of his wits, the beast charged me at an alarming rate of speed, leaping almost straight up into the air so that he could land on my back and dig his claws, jaws, and poison stinger into my unprotected flesh.

I quickly jumped sideways—setting off a few car alarms as I landed—turned around, dropped to my front knees, and raised my big elephant butt at the pouncing alien beast.

Now, before you interpret this move as a sign of submission, think again: What trumps an ant...besides a giant sneaker?

A spider. Ant-lion versus *elephant-spider!*

I raised my tail, exposing a massive set of spinnerets, and fired a tangle of web that would have impressed even Peter Parker.

The ant-lion fell to the pavement with a thud, bound up like a mummy. It growled at me in rage, wriggling helplessly in its silken straitjacket.

I knew I didn't have much time before the aliens regained their wits and decided to attack me themselves, so I quickly charged up to the ant-lion, knelt down, and probed through the sticky threads with my trunk to find the back of his armored head.

Then I undertook one of the more challenging telepathic adjustments I'd ever undertaken.

"I hope this works," I said, ripping the threads from its struggling body.

Fortunately, it did—the reprogrammed ant-lion quickly leaped to its feet, gave me a startled stare through his bulging bug eyes, and charged after the henchbeasts.

"Yeah," I yelled in booming elephant voice as they ran away into the woods. "You know that memory he had of *my* scent on his trainer's stick? Well, I kind of changed it to a memory of *your* scent, you ugly bugglies!"

But they were already too far gone to hear me. I could hear trees falling and their screams fading in the distance.

I morphed back into my usual handsome self just as Judy tentatively popped up her head from behind our Dodge minivan. Instead of Judy Blue Eyes, though, it was more like Judy Wide Eyes.

"Bet you didn't know I could do that, huh?" I said, kind of embarrassed.

"Yeah...No..." stammered Judy. "What was...? Who were...? Hey, why are we outside? Are you leaving?"

Watching her face was like seeing lights get shut off inside a building. I had no idea how, but Number 5 had clearly done something to her short-term memory. And if that was the case...well, this guy was getting more worrisome by the minute.

"Yeah, I better run, Judy," I said. "Stay out of trouble, okay?"

"Um, yeah," she said, waving like a Disney theme-park character as she walked, oblivious, back toward the restaurant. "Come back and see us real soon."

Chapter 34

I HOPPED BACK in the van but didn't get very far. Main Street was basically a two-mile-long parking lot. People were just sitting in their cars, staring into the bumper of the automobile in front of theirs, not the least bit worried about the plume of black smoke that was billowing farther up the road.

I turned the van into a levitating skateboard—like the one in that *Back to the Future* movie—and offered the young man in the Ford Focus behind me the sort of nod I imagined Danny Way would give before undertaking one of his record-setting jumps. Then I put my helmet on, jumped on the board, and zipped down the sidewalk to see what was going on.

A house was on fire—and in the most stunning show of community cooperation I'd ever seen in the U.S.

of A.—neighbors and passersby had formed a bucket bri-
gade to the house, filling and passing buckets, hand over
hand, to douse the flames. The place was a total loss, but
it looked like their efforts would at least keep the inferno
from spreading to any other properties.

"Where's the fire department?" I asked a businessman
standing in the line, sweating in his charcoal suit.

"Nobody's seen them in a month."

"What happened?!" I asked. "Isn't there any backup? I
mean, that's nuts!"

"I guess they're on vacation." The man passed along
another bucket.

I was flabbergasted. "Why didn't anyone call a nearby
town for help? Why hasn't this been all over the news?"

"They're on vacation too," he answered, and twitched a
little bit. "Everybody deserves a vacation."

"So Number 5 brainwashed you too, huh?"

"What?" asked the man, sweat dripping from his brow.

"Never mind," I said, shaking my head. And I put out
what was left of the fire with one giant alien breath, like
I was blowing out candles on a birthday cake. "Now go
home and take a shower."

Chapter 35

I'D LEFT LUCKY at the house with Mr. Gout—but one of the bigger problems with the telepathically adjusted is that, while they'll do what you tell them to do, they generally won't do what you've forgotten to tell them to do. Like taking the dog for a walk.

By the time I got home, poor Lucky was practically putting on a Number 5–style disco dance.

Since Mr. Gout had been diligently alienproofing the house for the past twenty-two hours, following the blueprints Dad had given him, I told him to go take a nap. Then I materialized a collar and leash and took Lucky for a much-needed stroll.

I don't know if you have a dog, but it's a real responsibility. I mean, they need to be fed, and they need to be walked, and if they make a mess on the sidewalk, you need to take care of that too.

Lucky seemed great and all, but I quickly decided that—after holding him back from chasing his third squirrel, and two neighbors' cats before that—until I had completely crossed every alien off The List, I couldn't possibly let myself be a dog owner.

Emma was going to kill me, but she and everybody knew that my responsibility here—to safeguard the Earth from a deadly alien scourge—was more important than providing a happy home for one dog. How did Mr. Spock put it? The needs of the many outweigh the needs of the few, or the one.

Especially when "the one" is a squirrel-chasing, cat-hating, car-barking, sidewalk-dookying dynamo of energy incapable of walking in a straight line.

And nearly incapable of being coaxed into a two-seater Ferrari—which is what I had to do...to make the four-mile drive to the local SPCA.

Chapter 36

I PARKED MR. GOUT'S Ferrari in front of a stenciled, rust-streaked OFFICE sign on the side of the first building we came to at the SPCA, not more than a mile from the TV transmission station we'd visited last night.

Lucky cowered on the passenger-side floor as I got out of the car and went around to open his door.

"Come on," I said, patting my legs in encouragement. "Come on, boy!"

He was having none of it. I conjured a tennis ball, then a doggy biscuit, then, finally, a piece of freshly cooked bacon, which did the trick. Lucky bounded out of the car just as a long-boned, white-haired woman in work boots, dark green pants, and a khaki shirt emerged from behind one of the sheds.

"Can I help you?" she asked.

She looked like Jane Goodall, that woman who studied apes in Africa, and she reminded me of somebody else I knew too, though I couldn't quite remember who.

"Um, we found a stray. No collar or anything, so—"

"Don't want him yourself?"

"I, um...my family is away a lot, and I have a full-time job, and—"

"Must be *some* job," she said, glancing disapprovingly at the Ferrari. "Bring him inside, and you can fill in some paperwork."

"Come on, Lucky," I said, materializing two more bacon bribes as the caretaker turned her back.

"You'll just need to fill in where you found him, and anything you've noticed about his health. I take it his hair was already singed before he made your acquaintance?"

"If you're thinking I—I mean, there's no way I—"

"A half dozen pups have come in these past few weeks with burns worse than that. I've called the police, but they say they haven't been able to find anything. I'll tell you, there's something very strange going on in this town. The way the dogs here bay all night, always in the direction of Old Man Wiggers' farm—"

"Old Man Wiggers' farm?"

"Right over that ridge," she said, pointing back into the woods. "I thought the crazy old coot had retired from farming, but, given the amount of noise he's been making, I guess he's reconsidered. Been driving the dogs and me crazy. Bulldozers, loudspeakers—I'd swear he's even been blasting with dynamite back there," she said, rubbing her eyes.

I glanced down at Lucky, who had finished his treat and was looking back up at me, tail wagging like crazy. "So, I, um, can just leave him with you?"

"This is the pound, and he's a stray, right?" Her penetrating blue-eyed stare was making me really nervous, like *she* was grokking *my* thoughts.

"You want to know what our euthanasia policy is, don't you?"

I nearly swallowed my Adam's apple. I was going to have enough trouble explaining this scenario to Emma and the gang without having to confront the fact that Lucky might get put down.

"The only thing we do to animals here is vaccinate, spay, or neuter. We hope they get adopted—because any dog will have a happier life with a loving forever home all its own—but we don't *kill* here."

"You ship them off someplace for that?" I said, tears welling. Forget "the needs of the many outweigh the needs of the one"—what kind of an alien monster *was* I?

"Any animal that comes here gets food, shelter, and veterinary care for the course of its natural life."

I nearly leaped across the counter and kissed her. I suddenly realized who she reminded me of: my alien grandmother, Blaleen. Another great lover of animals, although Blaleen was more into elephants than dogs.

This woman had also just reminded me that you humans can be about the best, most compassionate beings that have ever inhabited this particular dimension.

Chapter 37

OF COURSE, THE first thing Emma asked when I returned to the house was where Lucky was.

"Um," I said.

"Where *is he*?" she repeated.

Now my family and the rest of the gang were giving me subzero stares too.

"Well," I said, materializing a piece of bacon on top of Emma's left shoulder and telekinetically pushing open the kitchen door behind them.

Next thing we knew, Emma was pinned to the floor, giggling underneath a tail-wagging tornado of singed fur.

"Lucky! Stop!" she laughed as I mentally placed some bacon in her pockets. "You're tickling me!"

In the end, of course, I hadn't been able to go through

with it. I mean, I'm sure Lucky would have had a good enough life there at the SPCA, but I also knew what my grandmother would have thought of it, to say nothing of my friends and family.

"So I learned some interesting things today," I said.

"For starters, Dana, I need you to check out current and historical satellite maps of the area. There's a farmstead belonging to a Jarrod B. Wiggers a couple clicks east of where we were last night. I want you to scan recent images of the property to see what's changed there over the past few weeks.

"Emma and Willy, I need you to check Mr. Gout's hand-iwork here at the house and assess any weak points. We need the defenses to be tighter than a Tinkertoy in case any aliens decide to pay us a visit. Oh, and speaking of Mr. Gout, I sent him home."

"So you just let him go back to being a scumbag land-lord?" asked Dana.

"Well, I did give him one *slight* adjustment—I implanted a firm rule in his head that from this day forward he must be kind to his tenants and never charge them a penny more than what's fair.

"Mom, Dad, and Brenda," I continued, "please walk the neighborhood with Lucky and keep an eye out for any-thing strange, okay? I don't think Number 5's going to try anything just yet, but we know he's capable of surprises.

"And Joe, I need you to come with me to the van. We've got some theoretical physics equations to work through."

"Does it involve Avogadro's theory of spontaneous taco creation?" he asked hopefully.

"I think there are some Cool Ranch Doritos left in the back," I said.

"That'll do," he said.

Chapter 38

I SET JOE to work while I quickly dialed 411 for a McGillicutty residence on Mulberry Avenue. I didn't have the
nerve to call just yet, but I was half thinking about asking
Judy on a date...after I'd figured out a little more precisely
what kind of trouble Number 5 had been cooking up in
Holliswood and environs.

What Joe and I were doing is a little complicated to
explain in much detail, but I'll give you the basic idea: You
know how light travels really, really fast?

Well, in outer space, where stars and planets are so
far apart that the distance between them is measured by
how far light travels in a year, you start to see that light
isn't quite the greased lightning it's cracked up to be. In
fact, being unable to travel faster than light through space

would be kind of like cruising the interstate in a mule-driven cart.

Fortunately, alien technology has figured out some ways—which I won't attempt to explain right here—to surpass the speed of light.

That's not to say light's slowness doesn't have its uses. Like, for instance, when you want to *see into the past.*

Think about it. If light takes one hundred years to travel from Earth to Planet X—which is one hundred light-years away—then if somebody on Planet X has a really, *really* good telescope and wants to see what's happening on Earth right now, like you reading this book, for instance, then he'll have to wait one hundred years for the light that makes that image come to him.

And, if he were looking through his telescope right now, what he'd see instead of you reading this book is a picture of whatever was happening here *one hundred years ago.*

That's the core principle behind how my people—Protectors of the Universe that we once were—have been able to create a bunch of very good remote-control "telescopes" out in space. Some are ten minutes away, and some are ten million years away. By uplinking to them through the minivan's console, Joe and I were figuring out how to pull up a video feed of whatever had been happening on Earth from moments ago to millions of years ago—kind of like real-life TiVo.

My big idea was to get some clues about Number 5's plans by going back to when Number 5 and his hench-beasts first arrived in Holliswood.

"Um, Dan-o, what was that code you just read me? Zero-eight-five-three-five-six-F-zero-two-R-P, or zero-eight-five-three-five-six-F-zero-two-R-T?" asked Joe.

"Let's try whichever one you *didn't* just type in," I said as we received footage of a woolly mammoth playing with her baby in what looked like a prehistoric Holliswood Lake.

"I think that's a little too far back."

Chapter 39

"THAT'S IT," I said to Joe. "Play that scene right there."

He turned the dial and locked in the playback codes on our improvised deep-space historiscope. What we had before us was a pauseable, zoomable, playbackable recording of Number 5's arrival in Holliswood.

A pulse of light flashed in the sky over the pine forest next to a country road on the south side of town, and, in a microsecond, his fat, flabby, fishy self materialized, crackling with electricity among the burning pine trees.

Number 21 came next, and then, in a series of slow-motion lightning bolts, a handful, then dozens, then hundreds upon hundreds of alien henchfiends streaked down from the sky.

The fireworks ended with a dozen or so interstellar transport containers materializing in the midst of the horde.

Number 5 opened one and removed what looked like a small, neatly folded mesh of wires and circuits.

He unfolded it with his tentacles, carefully stretching it open to its full teardrop shape, and smiled.

"What is that?" asked Joe. "An alien-style fishnet stocking?"

I was in no mood to joke. "I think we have yet to witness the level of evil this creep is capable of," I told him as the real horror show began.

Chapter 40

WE WATCHED ON-SCREEN as Number 5 barked some orders at his minions, who quickly dispersed into the still-burning forest. Then he borrowed what looked to be a cell phone from Number 21, placed a call, and proceeded to wait impatiently in the middle of the road.

Four fire trucks soon arrived at the scene, squealing to a stop when they saw the big, levitating, tentacled catfish hovering in the middle of the road. Number 5 took advantage of the firefighters' astonishment and calmly glided up on the roof of the ladder truck. He twined a tentacle around the flexible communications antenna on top of the cab, and blue sparks coursed down its length.

A moment later, all the firefighters poured out of their trucks, in their black and yellow suits, and formed a

Macarena line as a camera crew of a dozen aliens came forward to film the dance.

The rest of the aliens returned, cheering and jeering from the edge of the burning forest as the mind-controlled firefighters slapped hands to the backs of their heads, then to their hips and gyrated.

The scene quickly shifted from absurd to abhorrent as a team of aliens advanced with unholstered blasters and began obliterating the dancing firefighters, one by one, melting them into slicks of black sludge as their film-crew colleagues zoomed in for close-ups.

The unabashed show of depravity made my insides burn. But Number 5 was clearly elated by the entire performance. He pumped his tentacle like he was Tiger Woods after making a tournament-winning putt.

When the last firefighter had been liquefied, Number 5 waved a "let's roll" gesture, and the aliens activated the hover-drives on the containers, hitching them to the backs of the fire trucks. Then, lights flashing, they drove off down the country road toward the edge of town.

Chapter 41

JOE ZOOMED OUT the view, and we watched as all but one of the alien-driven fire trucks pulled up to a nearby farm—no doubt the Wiggers' place.

Number 5's ladder truck had broken off from the others and was now headed into downtown Holliswood. It finally stopped off the main drag in front of a squat building with a big red neon sign on top: KHAW: HOLLISWOOD COUNTY'S PREMIERE NEWS TEAM.

Number 5 hovered off the truck and followed a dozen gun- and camera-toting aliens inside the TV station.

"It makes sense, right?" said Joe. "A free press is tyranny's greatest enemy. And Number 5's all about tyranny, so the first thing he does is go after the press."

"Yeah," I said. "Although I'm beginning to think there's

more to it than that. Say, TV signals travel at the speed of light too, right?"

"Right."

"Well, let's pick up the signal the station was putting out at this same moment. Can you do that?"

Joe made some adjustments, and in seconds we had a split-screen with what we could see of the TV station from the outside, plus what was on air at the time—Weatherman Ron, wearing a shiny suit, a black silk shirt, and tropical-print tie, pointing to a wavy red line on the map behind him.

"And if you thought it was hot enough for ya already, well, this mass of low pressure coming in from the west is gonna change whatchya think *hot* is. But first, it's going to bring us a whole mess of T-storms—*YOWZA!*"

He froze as a blue spark arced out of the remote control he used to toggle through his weather maps. And then LEN's "Steal My Sunshine" began to play, and he started to dance a spastic, Blues Brothers sort of dance, distorted laughter gurgling in the background.

He kept it up for thirty seconds or so, then Weatherman Ron disappeared in a bright blue flash of light. The off-camera laughter got louder.

"Did they just vaporize Weatherman Ron on *live TV*?" asked Joe.

I nodded, sadly.

"I mean, he was annoying and all, but *nobody* deserves that."

Chapter 42

THERE WAS SOMETHING very wrong with Gina Jensen, the news anchor. It looked like her hair had been nested in by squirrels, her makeup had been applied by chimpanzees, and her eyes had been replaced with giant marbles.

"HELLO, HOLLISWOOD," she spoke loudly and robotically. "WE AT *KHAW* HAVE SOME BREAKING NEWS TO REPORT. SOME VERY, VERY WONDERFUL BREAKING NEWS. SOME MONTHS AGO, HOLLISWOOD WAS CHOSEN BY SOME IMPORTANT FILM PRODUCERS TO BE THE LOCATION OF A VERY SPECIAL MOVIE. NO OTHER TOWN IN THE COUNTY, IN THE STATE, IN THE COUNTRY, IN THE WORLD WAS SELECTED.

WE SHOULD BE VERY PROUD AND DO EVERY-THING WE CAN TO MAKE THE FILMMAKERS COM-FORTABLE AND HAPPY. PLEASE BE SURE TO CHECK

YOUR CELL PHONES, TELEVISIONS, E-MAIL, AND TEXT MESSAGES REGULARLY OVER THE COURSE OF THE NEXT FEW WEEKS. IN FACT, YOU SHOULD BE SURE TO LEAVE ON EVERY DEVICE YOU OWN AT ALL TIMES—"

She twitched suddenly, and the camera panned left to the anchorperson sitting next to her.

Only it wasn't an anchor*person*...

There, in all his lard-butted alien repulsiveness, was Number 5.

Chapter 43

WHAT WAS IT with this guy? In my experience, Outer Ones tended to keep low profiles as they hatched their evil schemes, but here Number 5 was going out on the airwaves, totally flaunting his presence. He was either being stupidly overconfident or scarily calculating. And all the evidence I was finding was pointing toward option two.

"Joe, this broadcast was thirty-three days ago, right?" I asked.

"Right."

"So how did he manage to do this and not set off alarms all over town and even around the world? I mean, how does a big fat alien appear on TV in a modern American town and not have anybody even *notice?*"

"You mean besides the fact that nothing's too weird for

TV these days, and people probably think it's an ad for car insurance or something?"

"Right."

"Well, I've been running some scans and comparing broadcasts from nearby towns, and it looks like that by this point he had totally cut off Holliswood from the rest of the world. All the phone lines to the outside seem to be cut. The satellite dishes have been jammed. Even the power grid seems to have been interrupted."

"But how do the people on the outside not notice that the town's fallen off the map?"

"Number 5's a smart guy. Maybe he hacked into some nationwide communications network and figured out a way to jam the wider world's alarm bells or something. I don't know. Maybe he'll explain it in this speech he's about to give."

Chapter 44

JOE AND I turned up the volume and watched as our increasingly unpredictable foe addressed the town on live television.

"As the most important and powerful entity ever to set foot on your pathetic soil, I accept your town's obvious and unavoidable compliance with my delegation's mission. We could call it unconditional surrender, but, of course, you didn't put up enough of a fight for there to be a surrender.

"The point is that *you will do whatever I say.* I say 'jump'? You start jumping and wait for me to say how high in case I care to specify. I say 'sing,' you sing. I say 'check your mail,' you check your mail. Actually, ladies, you'll find a special gift in your mailboxes tomorrow that I want you to open right away.

"And if I say 'dance,' you *dance*. And let's try to do a little better job of it than Weatherman Ron. Wasn't he just *atrocious?* Here, let's practice — Gina, would you care to lead the town in our first-ever municipality-wide showcase? How about a little Justin Timberlake to get our toes tapping?"

The camera pulled back, and he began to clap his tentacles as "Rock Your Body" began to blast through the studio speakers. And then Gina and her producers climbed onto the horseshoe-shaped anchor desk and began a synchronized routine straight out of a Super Bowl halftime show.

I could faintly hear Number 5 laughing through the dance music.

"Joe, can you isolate Number 5's voice in the audio track, and filter out the music? Sounds like he doesn't realize he's getting picked up by the microphones."

"Easy-peasy," said Joe, patching in some algorithms. "It sounds like Fishy's conducting a separate broadcast back there."

"—true that the average human isn't worthy of being a slave on our home planets, but oh, how they can make us laugh! Welcome, viewers from Alpha Centauri to Zebulon Nexi. You are at this moment witnessing the very first minutes of the very first episode of the funniest live entertainment show in cosmic history!"

Just then the image on our monitor flickered and went blank.

"What's going on, Joe? Did we lose the signal?"

"I don't think so. It seems to be some kind of interference or—"

My heart nearly leaped into my mouth—the monitor winked back on, and there was Number 5, doing his old trick of looking right at me *through a television screen.*

"You *do* think I have a good chance at winning a Pulsar's Choice award, don't you, young Alien Hunter?"

How did he do it? How was he always a step ahead of me? How many other unguessed powers of his was I going to stumble upon? How many times was I going to have the feeling that not only was he toying with me, he was having me act from a script?

I fought an urge to put my frustrated fist through the monitor; I didn't want to completely lose my cool just yet. It was time to throw some attitude back his way.

"The only award you're going to win is when I drag your stinky, blubbery carcass down to the tackle shop and earn a trophy for the largest mutant catfish ever caught in North America."

"Are you calling *me* stinky, *Stinkyboy?*"

"How—" I started to say but stopped and punched the flat-screen display so hard my hand went straight through, and when I pulled it back, daylight was streaming in the hole. I'd put my fist right through the side of the van.

How did he know my childhood nickname? The nickname I'd had on my *home planet?!* How did he always seem to have everything *figured out?*

I grabbed the computer console and heaved it the length of the van at the back doors, where it exploded into a jillion fragments and set the van rocking like we'd run into a tree.

So much for not losing my cool.

Part Two

TWINKLE, TWINKLE, THEN YOU DIE

Chapter 45

I WAS SITTING with Mom at the kitchen table, pushing a spoon back and forth through my SpaghettiOs.

Usually I love SpaghettiOs for breakfast—they were almost the only thing I'd eat as a kid, back before I'd grokked the concept of gourmet cooking—but I didn't have much of an appetite right then.

"So, it sounds like Number 5's exploiting the population of this town for cheap entertainment," said Mom.

How many times did she have to go over the facts? I half considered dematerializing her, and I three-quarters considered saying something sarcastic about her keen powers of observation, but some instinct told me to bite my tongue and show some respect.

She was just trying to help, after all.

"Yeah, he's exploiting," I muttered. "And liquefying. And incubating."

Mom perked up. " 'Liquefying' I understand—but what do you mean by 'incubating,' Daniel?"

"He's gotten the women in the town to carry his eggs inside them."

"He *what?!*"

"Yeah," I said. "As near as the gang and I've figured out, it's not quite like they're pregnant, because his larvae are growing inside their stomachs. But it looks like he's determined that the expandability of the human female abdomen, combined with the human stomach's acidity, regular supply of food, and temperature, make for an ideal incubation chamber for his species' young."

"That's the most *sick*ening thing I've ever heard!" said Mom.

"You remember that tin of caviar you found in the mailbox? We ran tests on it in the van. Total DNA-match to Number 5. And hundreds of women around town are getting huge. And—get this—they've been 'pregnant,' they say, for just about four weeks.

"Which one hundred percent corresponds with when this 'caviar' appeared all over town. So Number 5 brainwashed them to eat it, and, voilà, he's got a couple jillion eggs getting nourished by the kind women of Holliswood."

Mom's jaw dropped. But she didn't even realize the full horror of it yet.

"Of course, we don't know what the end result's going to be," I continued. "Whether it'll kill the women or not."

Chapter 46

"DANIEL!" MOM RECOILED. "You've got to get to the bottom of this!"

"I know it, Mom," I told her. "It's just not turning out to be that simple. Every time we think we've set Number 5 back, it's like he's been expecting it. It's like we're acting a part in a play he scripted for us."

"So do something unpredictable. Improvise."

"We've tried that," I said, mushing a SpaghettiO flat with my spoon. "We've tried *everything*."

"Don't lie to your mother, Daniel. You haven't tried *everything*."

"Well, I mean everything *I can think of*."

"You haven't done that, either. You could try listening to your mother for once. Eat your soup. Little-known fact—SpaghettiOs aren't just comfort food, they're *brain* food."

"They are not."

"They are when *I* make them. And didn't I just tell you to start listening to your mother?"

I took a spoonful, and it was the weirdest thing—the fog instantly lifted from my brain. I began to see what clearly wasn't going to work, and where we might actually have a good chance against Number 5. Suddenly, where everything had been *im*possible, this entire mission seemed completely doable.

"Wow, Mom," I said, quickly polishing off the rest of the bowl. "What did you do to this stuff? I feel like an entirely new and improved Alien Hunter."

"Glad to hear it. I've always said there's nothing like a good meal to get a body back on track."

"Now, if only I could figure out how to get some more time to prepare our plans."

"Well, why don't you skip school, for starters?"

I don't care what planet you're from—you've got to love a mom who tells you it's okay to play hooky now and then.

Chapter 47

MOM HAD ME materialize an iPhone and promptly used it to call the administrative office at school.

"Hello," she said. "This is—" She put the phone on mute and asked me what surname I had used when I'd invented my school record.

"This is Daniel *Exley's* mother calling. I'm keeping him home today....What? You want to know why? Because I'm his mother and I say so, that's why....But that's ridiculous. Why would a parent not put their child's interest first and foremost? If I didn't have a darn good reason for keeping him home, *I wouldn't be keeping him home*....Sick? No, he's not sick, we just have something we need to solve here....

"Well, that's just plain silly. Honestly, I have never heard of anything so unreasonable. Let me ask you one more time, why would I—his *mother*—want to keep him home if not because I thought it best for him? . . . 'Against policy' my *ash*tray!

"You know what? You sound like the sort of person who would do really well as a midlevel bureaucrat in a totalitarian regime—then you could tell me straight out, 'Hey, lady, I don't make up the rules, I just blindly enforce them.' . . .

"*Personal?* You accuse me of getting personal, and you're telling me how to raise my son? Fine. You want *acceptable* reasons why Daniel's not coming to school? Well, stick these in your fascist helmet:

"Number ten: Daniel is attending an intergalactic symposium on ichthyological embryology today.

"Number nine: Daniel described your school as being a holding pen for the 'criminally underinspired.'

"Number eight: Daniel has developed allergies to fluorescent lights, number two pencils, and linoleum.

"Number seven: Daniel is locked in mortal combat with an electromagnetically gifted, levitating catfish from a planet eleven thousand four hundred light-years away.

"Number six: Daniel wrote an essay for his social studies class yesterday that was so good his teacher fainted, and we don't want to put any other educators in harm's way.

"Number five: We've looked over the terms of the No Child Left Behind Act and determined that if your school is doing the driving, we're okay with Daniel being left behind.

"Number four: Daniel's eyes glazed over so badly during yesterday's trigonometry class that he needs to go to the ophthalmologist today for a cleaning.

"Number three: Aliens have landed in Holliswood, and I think maybe we should reconsider our daily routine.

"Number two: Daniel's doctor fears that if Daniel has to hear one more nonsensical, bureaucracy-inspired edict come out of your office, he may decide to flee the country.

"Number one: If Daniel came in to school today, I would instruct him to find you and turn you into something more fitting for your personality... like a *potted plant*."

There was a dramatic pause.

"Would you believe it?!" she said, turning to me. "That nasty little person hung up on me!"

"It's okay, Mom. I think she probably grokked that I won't be showing up today."

"That's right. You've got more important things to do," she said, taking away my bowl and shooing me and Lucky out of the kitchen. "Now get going."

Chapter 48

I SPENT MOST of the rest of the day on The List, studying the reproductive habits of alien fish species and boning up on electromagnetic theory while my friends and family worked at their own parts of the puzzle.

Dad had the biggest breakthrough of the day by far.

"Daniel," he said, "I figured out how Number 5's been getting into the wiring. He's been broadcasting himself from nearby cell phone towers into any accessible electronic components, including the van and The List computer itself."

"So that's how he knew my childhood nickname, huh?"

"And that's how he's known where you've been almost every moment since you got here. He's essentially been hacking *himself* into any electronic device he pleases."

"That's just great. So if I ever want to get the jump on him, I have to give up the van, The List, and keep away from anyplace wired for electricity? I guess I'll just go wait in the woods and hope he happens to walk by."

"Sure, that's one way. Or you could just upload this decoy computer program I wrote into The List computer and leave it right here on the kitchen table. The program's designed to simulate your presence. So, when he checks in, he'll think you're right there in the room with the computer. Eating, surfing the Web, texting your buddies, doing your homework—"

"Homework? Don't you think that's a little unrealistic?"

"Well, you *look* like a geek," said Pork Chop.

"Hey, I'm *your* brother."

"Only in *your* imagination."

I shook my head and sent Dad off to upload the program. Maybe it would fool Number 5 for a little while and give me a chance to surprise *him* for once.

Dad came back at dinnertime to say all was ready and that the program would also show me sleeping when night came. After that, I dematerialized the rest of the gang, took Lucky for a quick walk, came back, cranked the new Green Day album, and spent some time in front of the bathroom mirror with a pair of scissors and a tube of superstrength hair gel. Mom had told me I needed a haircut, and I figured a talented guy like me shouldn't have much trouble doing something as simple as a haircut.

Once I'd perfected my new 'do, I drove my motorcycle to a small, blue-shuttered house on the north end of town.

The crickets were chirping like it was their last day on Earth, but otherwise everything seemed totally normal. Almost *too* normal.

I nervously pulled the silver elephant necklace from my pocket and hung it around my neck. Maybe it would bring me some luck. Then I cautiously approached the front door and rang the bell.

I heard footsteps and swallowed hard as the curtain on a window parted, revealing a brilliant blue eye.

I stood back, wondering if this was all a big mistake. The lock turned, and the door started to creak open. I threw out my right hand, firmly grasping the strange item I'd just materialized.

"What *beautiful* daisies!"

"You must be Judy's mom," I said, handing the woman the bouquet. "She has your eyes."

"Judy *said* you were sweet. Come on in. She'll be right down."

Chapter 49

JUDY'S PARENTS INVITED me to sit on the couch, and it was just like what you see in all the sitcoms and movies when the parents are meeting their daughter's date for the first time.

They seemed to be very nice, and I made sure to be polite and honest—well, without going into *too* much detail about my background—so I think I managed to make a pretty good impression. Judy's dad was an electrical engineer, so we definitely hit it off on that score.

We discussed computer chips, the latest developments in carbon-matrix superconductors, and a bunch of other supergeek stuff until Judy came downstairs. At that point—when I saw her in her summer dress with her hair down—I confess, I lost some of the thread of what Mr. McG was talking about.

"Look what Daniel brought you," said Mrs. McG, coming out of the kitchen with my flowers in a vase. "Aren't they beautiful?"

"And he's quite the budding electrical engineer, I can tell you," Mr. McG spoke up. "Really knows his stuff. I keep telling you, Judy, it's a real growth field."

"Such a well-mannered young man," chimed in Mrs. McG.

"Look, guys, he's *my* date, not *yours*. Come on, Daniel, let's go."

"I'll put your flowers in your room, dear."

"Thanks, Mom."

"And I'll find that copy of *Popular Wiring* I was talking about—the issue about lightning-proofing."

"That'd be great, sir."

"Okay, Mom and Dad. I'll be back by midnight."

"Have a good time," they said in one voice, holding hands as they beamed at us.

"Creepy, huh?" remarked Judy as we stepped out the door.

"They seem nice. And, um, healthy. Say, I'm going to go out on a limb and guess that you and your mom didn't get any caviar in the mail the other week."

"Oh, no, we got it all right. Can you believe it? Russian sturgeon are on the endangered species list, and our local news station decides it's a good idea to send the entire town tins filled with eggs that they ripped out of the bellies of pregnant fish. I totally e-mailed Al Gore about it."

"Actually, they weren't Russian sturgeon."

"Really? That's what it said on the label, didn't it?"

"Yeah, but you can't believe everything you read."

"Well, anyhow, I think fish eggs are a gross concept. I'm still glad I threw them away before Mom saw them. They can't be good for you anyhow."

"That's a safe assumption," I said, taking her hand.

Chapter 50

I MATERIALIZED AN extra helmet and helped Judy onto the back of my motorcycle.

"Where's a good place to eat in this town?" I asked through the intercom as we sped down her street. "Besides the diner, I mean."

"There's not a lot. There's one of those all-you-can-eat Lobster Hut places that my parents like, but I'm not really into seafood."

"That's understandable," I said, quickly logging onto the Internet. Another little perk of being an Alien Hunter is that I have wireless broadband connectivity...*in my head.*

There really wasn't much in the way of five-star restaurants in Holliswood. I took a few seconds to scroll through the customer comments on cityguide.aol.com and found that the At-Least-It's-Not-Monday franchise across from OfficeMax had the best reviews.

It wasn't exactly the sort of place in which you'd expect to bump into a *New York Times* food critic, but the HELP WANTED sign in the window gave me an idea, and I quickly summoned two characters from my imagination—Wolfgang, a chef trained at Le Cordon Bleu in Paris, and Jean-Luc, a headwaiter with the skill set of an employee of Le Cirque in New York.

They rushed in ahead of us, and the stunned manager hired them on the spot. Jean-Luc complimented a wide-eyed Judy on how much she resembled young Greta Garbo as he led us to a secluded table in the corner that was already set with starched white table linens and a floral arrangement that Judy said was the most beautiful she'd ever seen.

"I knew Thursday was 'Chicken Finger Night,' " she said as our third course, Canard à l'Orange, arrived at the table. "So I guess tonight must be 'Haute Cuisine Night.' "

"You should tell your friends."

"Are you sure you didn't have anything to do with this, Daniel?"

"Hey, if I had the kind of money to make something like this happen, would I be in Holliswood?"

"I guess not," she said, and laughed. "But I'm glad you are."

Whereupon I once again blushed as only an alien can.

Chapter 51

WE'D BEEN LOOKING forward to dessert but had eaten so much we couldn't possibly squeeze in another bite. So I gave Jean-Luc a handsome tip, and I took Judy for a ride in the country.

Judy wrapped her arms around my waist as we sped down back roads, losing ourselves in the confident drone of the engine and the buffeting, summer-perfect air. We drove for miles and miles, eventually stopping to look at some constellations from a distant field—I helpfully illuminated the lines between the stars so Judy could see the shapes more easily—and then, at her suggestion, we looped our way back to the King Kone drive-through near the high school.

"It's weird," said Judy, as she dismounted and took off her helmet. "This place is usually mobbed with kids. It's like *the* hangout. Jocks, stoners, goths, skate kids, sometimes even the World of Warcraft shut-ins."

"Maybe they heard homeschooled kids were starting to show up and decided it wasn't cool anymore," I said, earning myself a jab to the ribs I could have easily dodged but didn't.

The ice-cream stand itself was a tiny affair, more awning than building. It was basically just a counter area where the employees served the ice cream; a walk-in freezer; and the men's and women's rooms, which were accessible from outside.

We ordered a couple of soft-serve cups from the bored-looking counter boy and claimed a picnic table in the back, as far from the noisy road as we could get.

"Oh, darn," said Judy as we sat down. We'd failed to notice some chocolate sauce on the side of the table, and her dress brushed against it. "I'm going to get some soap and water on it so the stain doesn't set. Don't eat my ice cream while I'm gone."

I was pretty close to being done with my own already and shrugged.

She wagged her finger at me and headed inside, leaving me to find a cleaner table where I could contemplate my empty dish—and why her ice cream looked so much better than mine had.

I was just lifting a tiny spoonful to my mouth—pretty sure she'd never notice—when a blue flash lit up the ice-cream stand, and I heard the telltale blast of an alien firearm.

So I never did find out if her ice cream was any better than mine.

Chapter 52

I RAN SO fast I could hear napkins, empty Styrofoam cups, plastic spoons, and other litter getting sucked along in a vortex behind me.

I flattened myself against the outside wall of the ice-cream stand and took a quick peek inside the EMPLOYEES ONLY door. Two aliens were filming a couple of their friends lapping up some blaster sludge from the floor.

The counter boy's paper hat smoldered off to one side.

One of the aliens on the ground looked up at the cameras, human sludge dripping from his chin, and quipped, "I just love King Kone soft serve!"

The others laughed appreciatively. I slid back and, with my hand cupped over my eyes, stepped into the ladies' room.

"Judy," I whispered, putting my finger to my lips to quiet her.

"Daniel!" she screamed.

"I was kind of hoping you *wouldn't* do that," I said and threw her over my shoulder.

"What are you doing?!" she howled as we burst out into the night. I sprinted around the corner of the ice-cream stand and leaped the white plastic fence that separated the shop from the gas station next door.

I rounded the building and carefully lowered Judy to the ground. I forced myself to turn away as she smoothed down her dress, which had hiked up dangerously high on her legs as I carried her.

"What the heck was that all about?" she demanded.

I peered around the corner of the cinderblock wall and saw the aliens ransacking the ladies' room at the ice-cream stand, searching high and low for whomever had just screamed.

"Um, yeah. Sorry about that," I said. "I guess I like, um, memorable first dates."

Chapter 53

"DID YOU HEAR anything when you were in the rest-room?" I asked Judy.

"You mean besides you barging in? Hmm. Actually, I *did* hear a loud noise. Like a car backfiring or something. Totally startled me. What was it? Was the ice-cream stand *on fire?*"

"Um, back at the diner the other day, you know, when you made me the grilled cheese and pickle—and then out in the parking lot—do you remember seeing anything strange?"

"Strange, like..."

"Monsters? Aliens?"

"*What?!* Did you eat my ice cream? What's going on, Daniel?"

"Okay, look. Can we agree that there's a lot of weird stuff going on lately?"

She nodded vigorously.

"I mean, this isn't the first time something freaky's happened in recent weeks, right?"

She shook her head no.

"And there not being any kids here at the King Kone tonight? And the caviar in the mail? Or how people are watching even *more* TV than usual? And the fact that the firemen have all disappeared, but nobody talks about it?"

"Yeah, I guess that's all weird enough."

"Well, remember that story I told you about how I was an alien?"

"Yeah, that was a little bizarre ... but cute. I feel like an alien in this town myself."

"Well, what if I told you it's true?" I began, and then I couldn't stop. "And that the stuff I was telling you about there being other aliens around here is on the level too? And that I've figured out the evil alien that I'm tracking right now has learned how to get into everybody's heads and keep them from realizing, or at least remembering, that anything's wrong—even when they've seen it with their own eyes?"

I took a deep breath, half expecting Judy to turn and run away from me as fast as she could. But she still had her incredible eyes fixed right on me.

"I guess I'd say you could probably tone it down with the stories. I mean you *did* get me out on a date—I'm a homeschooled kid, remember, so I'm just a little desperate—so you really don't need to try so hard. Say, cool elephant necklace. Is that Indian?"

She put her hand on my shoulder and leaned in close as if to look at it, but she seemed to be aiming her gaze more at my lips than at my neck. My heart jumped up in my chest—was she about to—I mean, were *we* about to—?

I never found out because, right then, there were a bunch more bright blue flashes and a huge explosion.

Chapter 54

WE CAREFULLY PEERED around the wall again and saw that the aliens—frustrated by not being able to find their potential victim—had decided to destroy the ice-cream stand. Not to mention my motorcycle. There was nothing left but a smoking hole in the ground, and the fiends were now staggering around the lot, firing into the air like a bunch of drunk banditos in a bad spaghetti Western.

"Daniel—those are—"

"Yeah, I know. Aliens. Bad aliens. And you know what? As soon as you turn away, you're going to forget you ever saw them."

"Nuh-uh," she said, on the verge of tears. "I'll never forget seeing this for as long as I live."

"Oh yeah?" I asked, pulling her back to look at me.

"Huh, what?" she said. "Did we just kiss? 'Cause it

must have been pretty good. Seriously, Daniel, I feel like I must have blacked out or something. Wow. Here, let's do it again—"

She leaned toward me, but, instead of kissing her, I put my hands up to her face and did a little scan on her brain.

Sure enough, right there in the middle was this weird little electrical imbalance—a sort of hovering charge within the nerves of the short-term memory area.

So that's how Number 5 had done it. He'd implanted some sort of semi-intelligent electrical impulse—like a computer program—in her head that apparently kept her from retaining any memories that involved experiences with aliens.

"Hey," she said, "that feels nice, but do you want to kiss me or not?"

"Um, yeah," I said, and we kissed. And though it took all my strength to stay focused, I managed to blast a carefully formed countercharge directly into her mind.

"Ow!" she yelled, pulling back from me and putting her hand to her lips.

"I'll say," I said. "Sweater shock, I guess."

"Yeah, but you're wearing a T-shirt. And we're not standing on a rug. And it's *June*."

I shrugged.

"Daniel, this is all so weird."

"You want weird?" I said. "Look around the corner at what's going on over at King Kone."

"What? Here, let me see—"

She saw at least three of the aliens piling into their stolen KHAW-TV news van.

"Oh my gosh! Aliens!"

"Yeah, *aliens*—in other words, let's get the heck out of here ASAP!"

Chapter 55

AFTER I FIXED Judy's memory, I was hoping she'd be a *little* scared of Number 5's blaster-toting thugs—at least enough to want to step out of the way and let aliens fight aliens.

But she wasn't afraid in the least. She was *angry*. And she was determined to convince me to let her help.

"What do you mean, let's *get out* of here? We can't let these monsters take over the town!"

"Okay," I finally relented after ten minutes of arguing with her, "but we're just watching for now. And you need to listen to everything I say, okay? I say 'get down,' and you hit the deck, right? I say 'run,' you run like there's a flesh-eating monster right behind you, okay? And if we get separated for any reason, you go right back to your house and take care of your parents, okay? And *no* touching TVs or cell phones or computers or anything electronic, okay? I'm positive that's how Number 5 got into your head in the first place."

"Aye-aye, Captain Daniel!"

"I mean it."

"I know you do. But isn't it kind of a moot point? I mean, didn't they just drive off?"

"Oh, that," I said, snapping my fingers and rematerializing my motorcycle. I also made us two new helmets—one blue and one pink, just like her dress.

"Awesome," said Judy, grabbing the blue one. "It goes with my eyes."

Chapter 56

WE FOLLOWED THE KHAW van at a safe distance into downtown Holliswood and back to the television station.

We parked at the top of the four-story public garage across the street.

"Here," I said to Judy, "stand back a bit. We need something a little better at eavesdropping than our own eyes."

"Like, ears, maybe?" Judy quipped.

"Better," I replied, and turned my bike into Dad's minivan.

"Wow," said Judy. "Can you make *anything*?"

"Anything I can grok," I said.

"Huh?"

"It means 'understand,' roughly. I guess you haven't been reading any Robert A. Heinlein."

"If he wrote after 1920 and was fun in any way, the

answer's no. I just got done with *Silas Marner*. Talk about Snoozeville."

"Yeah," I said as we climbed inside the minivan. "They use that book to punish criminals on my home planet. They make the worst offenders read it out loud and then write reports about the author's use of symbolism and metaphor."

"Ouch. Say, is that a *gun*?" asked Judy, pointing at an RJ-57 over-the-shoulder tritium-charge bazooka that was latched in the munitions cabinet at the back of the van.

"Yeah, and it's powerful enough to punch a hole right through Mount Rushmore," I cautioned. "So stay away from it, okay?"

I noticed Judy didn't make any promises.

"Here, let's fire up the van's eavesdropping equipment," I suggested, "and figure out what those space bullies are doing."

The flat screens winked to life—I'd replaced the one I'd punched my hand through the other day—and scanned around to see what was going on inside the station's walls.

I didn't detect Number 5's massive electromagnetic signature anyplace, but there were at least forty of his regular, low-level henchbeasts in there, including the handful that had just returned from the ice-cream stand.

I also discovered that they were already transmitting the raw footage of the ice-cream stand incident to their network in outer space.

We watched as the counter boy put down the phone and began juggling ice-cream scoops and chanting, "I scream, you scream, we all scream for ice cream!" And then got melted. And eaten.

Judy gasped in disbelief. "So this is the kind of inhumanity we're dealing with here..."

"Judy, you don't have to do this," I warned her. "I'm telling you, that's only a fraction of what these guys are capable of."

And it was nothing compared to what came next.

Chapter 57

A LOCAL WOMAN was slogging slowly back to shore from the middle of a shallow farm pond in her soaking-wet nightgown.

The camera panned right, and an alien carrying a long-handled net went splashing out into the pond behind her. He sprinkled a can of fish food, waited a moment, and scooped the net through the water, hoisting it up in the air, waving his fist triumphantly as he did so.

The camera zoomed in on the wriggling net, revealing a mass of two-inch-long, fat-bellied baby fish that promptly emitted a series of bright blue sparks, which caused the alien to jerk and jolt... and fall back, quite dead, into the water.

Now the camera zoomed back and panned left, bringing into focus the pond's shoreline, which was crammed with spectator aliens. In the center, Number 21 and Number 5 were standing on some sort of viewing platform.

The former was passing the latter a cigar and then offering to light it as the aliens around cheered and stomped their feet.

"What were those things in the net?" asked Judy. "Electric eels?"

"More like electric alien catfish," I said, "and the direct descendants—if not clones—of the fifth most powerful alien on Earth."

We watched as the woman crawled out of the pond and onto the shore. One of the aliens gave her a new tin of caviar and a can opener. A half dozen others slapped her back in mock congratulation. The camera zoomed in on her face, and I realized I'd seen her zombie-like mug before—she was the pregnant woman who'd refused my help at S-Mart.

She vacantly nodded at the aliens and trudged up the hill toward town, eating the contents of the can as she walked.

Judy gasped in horror.

Truth be told, I did too.

Chapter 58

I SHOOK MY head. "How many women do you figure there are in Holliswood, Judy? A couple thousand?"

"Easy," said Judy.

"And how many eggs do you figure there are in a tin of caviar? A thousand or so?"

"Sounds right."

"So a thousand times two thousand is, um, a couple million. And if they do this every month or so—"

"You can't possibly mean—?!"

I nodded sadly.

"That's so disgusting, so sick, so *wrong!*"

"So evil," I added. "Yeah, the world may just be on the verge of the biggest alien invasion in history. And it's going to be homegrown."

Just then the equipment picked up a new audio signal.

It was coming from the station's control room and an operator someplace up in space.

"Boy, did you see the jolt that thing gave that poor goon?" said the voice from the control room. "They really look like they're going to be chips off the old block."

I aimed the wall-penetrating camera at the control room and—just as I'd suspected—confirmed that it was Number 21, in all his sweaty, white-haired monkeyosity.

"So tell me, are you guys bulking up enough on crew?" asked the voice from space. "It'll be one thing to have a few thousand Number 5s around, but who's going to do the heavy lifting?"

"No worries," said Number 21. "We've had the troops on a strict breeding diet since we arrived. Here, just watch the rest of this feed, and you'll stop worrying about that end of things."

Judy and I watched too—at least as much as we could without getting sick.

A hunch-shouldered henchbeast sitting in a stiff-backed chair was sipping at a can of motor oil. An off-camera voice told it to remove its shirt.

The camera moved around behind it so that we could see a bulge containing no fewer than two dozen baby henchbeasts—*they were growing right out of the creature's back!* And, right then and there, several of the offspring took advantage of the lifted shirt to separate from their parent's flesh and leap to the floor.

The next scene was from a chicken coop filled with hundreds upon hundreds of the henchbeast offspring, leaping and clinging to the arms and legs of an overburdened alien parent who was attempting to refill a trough with motor oil.

"If they can breed that quickly..." Judy started to say.

"Yeah," I continued, "this planet's toast."

Chapter 59

SO THAT WAS Number 5's plan. And a darn good one too... I mean, if your objective is to generate close to two billion hours of exploitative entertainment and destroy an entire species in the process.

Well, at least I could cross four more items off the mystery board:

1) *Why had Number 5 picked relatively weak, unintelligent henchbeasts as his primary helpers?* Because this particular species happened to replicate and grow to adulthood faster than any other in the cosmos, meaning Number 5 would be able to breed a big enough goon squad in time to get his show on the air for the next intergalactic network season.

2) *What was the deal with all the motor oil I'd seen the aliens stealing and guzzling?* Nothing has more easily digestible raw calories for this species—useful for rapidly growing babies, and their parents—than motor oil.

3) *Why were the aliens always lapping up the sludge left behind by their melted human victims?* Because, while it's high in calories, a diet of motor oil is lacking in certain essential vitamins and minerals, whereas a melted human body has lots of essential nutritive ingredients needed for raising healthy aliens.

4) *What was the deal with the fish food the women had been purchasing at S-Mart that day?* They'd been taking it to feed the baby Number 5s they were raising in the fish ponds at Wiggers' farm.

So now I just had a few dozen remaining questions to answer. Questions, you know, like, was there a weakness in his plan?

Personally, I was starting to have doubts.

"Judy," I said, "let's get you home now, okay?"

She didn't say anything, which I thought was strange. But not as strange as what I saw when I turned to speak to her—because there was nobody there.

Chapter 60

"WHERE THE—?!" I started to say, but then I spotted her—on one of the van's monitors. She had taken the bazooka and was running across the road between the parking garage and the TV station.

No time to waste chasing to her, so I decided to teleport myself instead. It's a skill Dad had me practicing lately. I really had to grok where it was I needed to go, and it required way more focus than I could usually pull off near the clutches of an alien . . . but right now, Judy was running straight into a death trap, and there was only one thing I cared about.

I materialized on the sidewalk in front of her and—as gently as possible, of course—tackled her and shoved her into the hedges in front of the station.

"Are you crazy?!"

"Let go of me, Daniel."

"You think you can run over here with a gun and take on the twenty-first-most-powerful alien on the planet—and who knows how many of his goons—just like that?"

"You said yourself it was a pretty powerful gun."

"Yeah, well, if you can get them to agree to stand in a straight line and not move while you squeeze the trigger, sure, you might have a chance. But there's a bigger chance they'd turn that thing against you."

"But you were just sitting there watching and listening, and every single passing minute these monsters are getting a little closer to taking over not just Holliswood but the whole planet! You said so yourself!"

She was like a tiger trying to wrench herself out of my grasp to keep running. Then, all at once, she went limp under my weight and looked at me sadly. "I know you don't have any family left to save . . . but *I* have mine."

I couldn't think of anything to say to that.

"I mean, if you could go back in time and have another chance to save your parents, wouldn't you?"

"Look, Judy, you can have all the powerful weapons in the world, but if you don't have a plan—and if you don't know what you're getting into—you won't have a snowball's chance in Atlanta.

"If there's one thing I've learned in fighting evil aliens, it's that it's very important to do some serious homework. You see, with tests like this, there are no makeup exams. You fail, and that's the end."

"But with your powers . . ."

"My powers are only as good as my imagination. And my imagination is only as good as what I've learned. That's why I have to study things really hard. If we bide our time, we'll have a better chance."

"Prove it, Daniel," Judy demanded, but her steely blue eyes softened a little now.

"Okay," I went on, secretly admiring her negotiating skills. "Since I have the sense that you aren't going to go home quietly unless I prove what I mean, let's at least leave the gun here and sneak inside so I can show you something that will change your mind, okay?"

"And if you're not right, you give me back the bazooka — plus a platoon of Navy SEALs — to help me bust in through the front door."

She looked me in the eye, and we both started to smile.

"But if you *are* right," she went on, "what do you get from *me*?"

"Then I get to take you home and, um, you have to go about your life like normal till I give the sign, okay?"

"That's it?" she asked, leaning in close. "You can't think of anything else you might like?"

And so we made out right there in the bushes in front of the alien-infested TV station.

And while I'm not an Alien Hunter who's in the habit of kissing and telling, I made up my mind — next time I saw her in her diner uniform — to change her name tag from "Judy Blue Eyes" to "Judy Mind Blower."

Chapter 61

WE SNUCK INTO the station through the freight entrance at the back of the building.

The first thing we noticed was that the place smelled like a zoo—a zoo at which the cage cleaners had been on strike for a week. It's a well-documented fact that personal hygiene is a really low-priority item for the Outer Ones, but it never fails to take my breath away when I go somewhere they've been—especially if the windows haven't been left open.

I had to make us invisible twice as patrolling hench-beasts scuttled past, but we found our way to the alien-built central server core on the second floor without too much trouble.

I quickly sat down at the administrator's terminal and brought up a blinking holographic map of the world, which spun slowly in the center of the room. Every village, town, and city on Earth was labeled in successively wider rings of color radiating from the tiny red bull's-eye that was Holliswood, ending in a big blue circle that covered the backside of the planet.

Each color zone had a countdown clock on it. Holliswood's was counting down below 73 hours now, while the next ring was counting down from 273 hours, the one after that 473 hours, the one after that 673 hours…all the way to the last at 4,473 hours, which corresponded to about six months from now, the equivalent of an intergalactic broadcast season.

"I knew it," I said. "This town is just the pilot episode."

"So this is just the beginning…" Judy echoed.

"And in a matter of months, they will have filmed the demise of every single human settlement on the planet, from New York City to the smallest fishing village on the Indian Ocean."

"Okay, but there's something you haven't thought about," Judy challenged. "If these goons are, like, doubling their population every few days, how's the chief alien going to control them all? You said he's the director—and directors are the ones who make the shows work, right? All those aliens are going to need somebody to tell them how to run each location, and he can't very well get to over a thousand cities in a single day…can he? I mean he sure doesn't *look* like Santa Claus."

"Well, Sherlock, that's the reason he has the women of Holliswood coughing up his babies in that pond."

"So I guess *his* kids must grow pretty fast too. But can they become smart enough to run a filmed invasion that quickly?"

"I don't know exactly how it's possible, but I bet he's figured that out too. I think I may have seen some training equipment that will let him manage that end of things."

"Okay, Mr. Alien Smarty Pants, so is that what you wanted to show me?" Judy asked, sounding skeptical. "I mean, still, won't it be harder to put these guys out of business when there are millions of them, rather than just hundreds, like right now? Shouldn't we go ahead and attack before they've bred?"

"Well, there's one more thing," I said, typing in a code. The display in front of us briefly flashed "Emergency Abort Test 2," and then a crowd of shoppers dancing the Electric Slide in some grocery store checkout lines appeared on-screen.

After about fifteen seconds, the music was interrupted by Number 5's voice. "Very nice! Now stop dancing," he said, and began to laugh. "And, now...stop *breathing*."

First one fell, then another, then dozens of victims collapsed to the floor. I fast-forwarded so we didn't have to watch the whole horrible thing but stopped where a hench-beast walked out, kicked a couple of the bodies, and gave a thumbs-up.

"Ex-cellent," Number 5 chortled.

I stopped the playback. How could any intelligent being be so twisted? I mean, I guess I'd seen evil before, but the fact that he was doing this just for laughs...

"So you mean—?" asked Judy.

"Yeah, he can make people die at his command."

"Including my parents?" she asked, drawing a deep breath and wiping her eyes.

I nodded.

"Promise me you're going to stop him, Daniel."

"I promise *we'll* stop him," I said. "Now let's get out of this place and get you home."

Chapter 62

"LOOKS LIKE WE made it with three minutes to spare," I said as we pulled up in front of her house.

"What? My curfew, you mean? Now there's a joke. Here, let's go for a walk," she said.

"I'd like nothing better, Ms. Blue Eyes, but this is our first date, and I don't want to get off on the wrong foot with your parents, and, anyhow, there's kind of this alien invasion going on that I've been entrusted with shutting down and—"

The front door opened, and Mr. and Mrs. McGillicutty rushed out onto the porch.

"Did everything go okay?" asked Judy's mom, clutching her husband's arm nervously and looking accusingly at her daughter. Mr. McG seemed pretty agitated himself.

"We had a great time," said Judy, annoyance starting to cloud her concern for her parents.

"Are you sure?" asked Mr. McG.

"What's the matter with you two?" asked Judy. "I'm back before curfew, aren't I?"

"Well, that's just it, dear. How good a date could you have been if he got you home before curfew?! Daniel, was she rude? Did she remember to say please and thank-you?"

"Your daughter is the loveliest, smartest, bravest girl I've ever had the privilege of taking on a date, Mrs. McG."

It was Judy's turn to blush.

"Well," said Judy's mom, and she and her husband immediately brightened. "Well, in that case—I mean we're not trying to rush you or anything—but we want to let you know we're really laid back, and you don't need to come to Mr. McGillicutty and formally ask for her hand. Whatever you two are comfortable w—"

"*MOM!!!*"

"What, dear? I just want to lay things out there for Daniel's benefit—"

"You guys homeschooling me in academics is one thing, but telling me how to conduct my social life, and talking to me about *marriage*—!"

"Don't yell at your mother, Judy. We just happen to have some experience with these things, and when the right person comes along, well, you can just tell."

"That's right, Dad, *I* can tell. *You* don't need to tell me in front of a date and embarrass me beyond all reason."

"But Daniel here's such a terrif—"

"Actually, I'm not as perfect as you guys might think," I said, backing slowly down the stairs. "I mean, I really have my share of issues. I've had trouble maintaining a fixed residence—"

"I could clear out the rooms above the garage for you," suggested Mrs. McG. "There's even a working shower over there—"

"And I regularly find myself cavorting with disreputable types. *Really* disreputable types—"

"Look, he's even self-effacing!" said Judy's mom.

"They're right, honey," Mr. McG relented, winking at his wife. "Let's stay out of this. Why don't we go to the kitchen and rewash some dishes so that we're out of their hair and they can have their space?"

"Oh, okay. Right," said Judy's mom, giving her own subtlety-free wink back at her husband.

"I'm so sorry about them," whispered Judy as they went back into the house. "Actually, I'm mortified."

"Don't worry about it," I whispered back. "I expect Number 5's recent mind games have affected their social boundaries a little is all. The brain's a delicate organ, you know. Probably when he zapped them, he caused some unintentional side effects. Like making them desperate for you to get married to an alien," I explained, thinking that he probably didn't intend for them to pick *this* particular alien.

"Gosh, I hope you're right. My life is *over* if they're going to treat my dates like this. Not that I can imagine dating anybody but you, of course. Daniel, I really did have a wonderful evening, even if it did mostly revolve around those nightmarish aliens."

I probably would have blushed even if she hadn't given me a kiss right then, but she did, and my head nearly burst with happiness.

"I can't believe those aliens want to make a comedy of us," she said.

"The Divine Comedy, maybe," I babbled.

"Aw, you're so sweet," she said, and gave me a kiss I'll remember for the rest of my life.

Chapter 63

"YOU OKAY BACK there?" I asked through the helmet's intercom.

"You're going a little fast, aren't you?" she asked.

"You haven't seen anything yet," I said, briefly popping a wheelie, and bringing the speedometer up to 110 miles per hour.

I was elated. It was a beautiful day, and I finally had a solid theory about how I might possibly stop Number 5.

Also, I was alone with one of my favorite people in the whole universe.

"Stop squeezing so hard, Dana," I said. Taking Judy along this morning to check out Number 5's farm had been out of the question, of course—because of my vow never to imperil any humans, and my need to concentrate.

"Well, slow down! You're making me wish we'd gone to school instead."

"*School*—I totally forgot!" I said. "This could be a problem."

I pulled the bike over, and we took off our helmets.

"What's the big deal?" asked Dana. "We've only been once. You think they're going to miss us?"

"The problem is that we're on the books now. And if they don't get a call, and I don't show up, they may have a truant officer stop by the house. And if a truant officer goes out to the house and finds nobody there, he may call it in on a radio or a cell phone. If he does that, Number 5 may just pick up the signal and wonder what's going on. Because, you see, Dad's program, if it's working, has been fooling him into thinking I'm there. And this could blow that cover."

"I guess you're pretty smart anticipating a problem like that," said Dana, one hand on her hip and the other extended toward me, her finger and thumb pinched together. "But clearly you're not so smart about other things."

"What's that?" I asked, and swallowed nervously as I saw that she was holding a long black hair.

"Been riding around with somebody with wavy black hair, Daniel? *This* was on the collar of your motorcycle jacket."

"Oh, um, that, well...you know I really better get Mom here to deal with that truant officer situation, so, sorry if this seems sudden—"

I dematerialized Dana and took a deep breath before summoning Mom.

In some ways, this girl business was *way* more complicated than hunting aliens.

Chapter 64

"MOM," I SAID. "Here's your iPhone. Do you think you could call your friend at the principal's office and tell her I'm sick?"

"Of course, honey," she said, and happily dialed the school's attendance line.

"Yes, this is Mrs. Exley calling again—Daniel's mother?...Fine. How are *you* today?...That's wonderful. And your *policies?* How are they?...What do I mean? I mean if you were a normal person, I might ask about your family, but it seems clear to me that school district policies are what's closest to your heart...

"Well, that's all very interesting, but actually this isn't a social call. I'm just following up to say that Daniel's staying home today.... No, it's for none of the reasons he stayed home yesterday.

"Today, you see, he's quite sick.... You need his doctor's name, you say? No problemo. You have a pen? I'm going to warn you, he has more than one disease, and we're seeing a bunch of different specialists today.

"Number ten: He is being treated by Doctor Yuri Fishman for voltaic catfish fever.

"Number nine: He's seeing Doctor Yvonne Yurmunni for interstellar impecuniosity.

"Number eight: He has an appointment with Doctor Darth Crater for his space pox vaccination.

"Number seven: He's receiving aromatherapy from Mindy Fresh, MD, for his acute aversion to extraterrestrial halitosis.

"Number six: His localized academic malaise is being reviewed by Dr. Inogono Takit.

"Number five: S. Hugh Striker, MD, is counseling him about his obsession with lists.

"Number four: Dr. Wei-Goh Holmes is treating him for an especially nasty strain of domestic nostalgiasitis.

"Number three: Dr. I. M. Trubbell is assessing the state of his bureaucratic mumbo jumbo allergy.

"Number two: Dr. Slobodan Sonne is seeing him about his accelerated bipedal locomotion.

"Number one: Hello? Are you still there? ... Daniel, I think she hung up on me."

"She probably just needed one excuse, Mom, but thanks."

"No worries, Daniel. I just figure the best way to teach

people like that a lesson is to overload them with whatever it is they think they want."

"Interesting thought, Mom," I said, sending her home with a blink of my eye and summoning Dana. We pulled back onto the road and headed off to meet Number 5.

Chapter 65

I BEGAN BY doing what any highly disciplined military commander would do on the eve of battle—I ate a four-course meal.

Dana and I had climbed a hill above a cornfield opposite the Wiggers' property. I'd made us a picnic including wasabi-crusted salmon fritters, chanterelle-and-pork-medallion panini, watercress salad, vichyssoise, and a carafe of Gatorade.

"So what were you doing last night, Daniel, off on your own like that?"

"I was just confirming some theories I've been working on. Some light reconnaissance, you know, stuff like that."

"By yourself?"

"Um, pretty much, yeah."

"Pretty much?" she asked. "And that black hair I found

earlier probably just happened to land on your collar? Just had been blowing around in the wind?"

I guess dematerializing her hadn't made her forget. "Hair?" I said incredulously. "What hair?"

"The one that looked just like this other one that I found in your blue motorcycle helmet and which *isn't mine or Emma's.*"

"Wow," I said turning the hair into a butterfly that flew from her grasp. "Is that a tiger swallowtail?"

"You aren't going to distract me so easily. Whose hair was that?"

"Just a kid I met at the diner," I said, thinking quickly. "Number 5's goons had given her a rough time, so I just checked in on her."

"Sure you did."

"And she gave me some good information too. Turns out Number 5's programmed everybody in this town with some sort of standing electronic charge that lives inside their heads. Makes them conveniently forget things they've seen; makes them responsive to his orders—stuff like that."

"And she told you this?"

"Well, no, but I did figure out how to remove the charge from her head, so that now—provided she stays away from TVs, computers, and cell phones—she's once again in control of her own mind."

"Sounds like it must have been a pretty *intimate* procedure."

"Sure, I mean, I had to basically go inside her brain

and.... Wait, I know what you're thinking. But you know I'd never get emotionally involved with any humans. I mean, it's just not fair—"

"So you were just *using* that poor girl? She was nothing but an experiment?"

I shook my head. This clearly was not something to get into with Dana.

"Let's just eat our lunch and relax, okay, Dana? It's a gorgeous day, and we've got a big afternoon ahead of us."

She bit into her sandwich with a little more force than was necessary.

I sighed and looked around at the rolling hills, the brilliant blue sky, the butterflies and birds flitting around the field below.

"This really is a beautiful planet, isn't it?" I said. "So much diversity, so much that's lovely and good. You know, that's what really gets me about the Outer Ones. I mean, if I had to come up with a definition of evil, I'd say it's not just not appreciating beauty but wanting to mess with it, control it, own it.

"I mean, this whole show Number 5's aiming to make—it's all about taking this fantastic human species and bending it to his will for nothing more than cheap entertainment. A true artist would document them. Would present humans and their planet in all its glory—the plays they've written, the beautiful art they've made, the cities, the fields..."

"Put a sock in it, Daniel; (a) I'm not forgetting that you

went on a date last night, and (b) you have a crumb on your lip, and it's driving me crazy. Here, let me take it off."

"Oh, okay, sure," I said, leaning forward so she could remove it. I just didn't expect she was going to do it with her lips.

Chapter 66

A GUY'S GOT to give his imagination some credit when a girl he's dreamed up manages to make him dizzy with a kiss.

"Wow," I said. "That must have been some crumb—"

We began kissing again. The blue sky and green fields were twirling around like I was in a music video.

"I'm not exactly complaining," I said, "but what was *that* for?"

"Must be that hot new hairdo of yours, spike. Or that new bling," she said, fingering my necklace.

"Hey," I said, "you're supposed to be my dream girl."

"So?"

"So dream girls just say no to unnecessary sarcasm."

"Having dreams is one thing," said Dana. "Controlling them is something else."

"I guess they're kind of like reality that way," I said, and, as if on cue, seven henchbeasts, who must have been crawling on their bellies toward us through the tall grass, sprung up, grabbed Dana, and rushed off toward the woods, depositing her in the arms of a big sweaty space monkey.

Chapter 67

"HOLD IT, SHE'S not even real!" I yelled. "I just make her up. With my imagination!"

I leaped to my feet and scanned the area for whatever sort of booby trap Number 21 had laid for me.

"You make her up, huh?" he said, snorting through his ugly snout, and passing Dana to his henchbeasts. "In that case, I guess let's *make believe* my soldiers are *breaking her arm*."

The henchbeasts looked back at him like confused children.

"Break. Her. Arm," he said, and now they all nodded and positioned themselves to snap her left arm.

In a flash I gave Dana a wink and turned her into a thirty-five-foot anaconda, which promptly wrapped itself around their necks and squeezed. Hard.

"Didn't believe me, did you?" I asked Number 21 as his henchbeasts fell to the ground, their heads swelling like balloons.

"Oh, I *believed* you. I just wanted to keep you distracted while I got *this* ready."

He was suddenly aiming the same shockwave cannon he'd used to knock me unconscious in S-Mart.

"Oh," I said, as he pulled the trigger.

Chapter 68

LIGHTNING QUICK, I reached down, tossed up a handful of dirt, and mentally forced the particles into a shield.

Number 21 started to laugh, but the blast completely deflected around me. I took some pleasure watching that obnoxious ape lower his gun and scratch his head.

"What else you got?" I yelled across the field at him.

He dropped his weapon, and one of his cronies passed him a gun so large I was kind of surprised he was able to hold it. I wasn't familiar with the type, but it was so big it looked like it could have blown apart a modest-sized asteroid.

"And what do *you* have, my little *Stinkyboy*?" he asked, his voice dripping with condescension.

"Better a stinky *boy* than a stinky *space ape*," I said, reaching dramatically to my side and unholstering my weapon of choice—my hand with my index and middle finger extended, my thumb cocked like a pistol's hammer. "Nanny-nanny boo-boo!"

He laughed like a hyena.

"They said you were a character, but it's truly a shame that your curtain call is coming so soon."

"You're too kind," I said. "Shall we draw on the count of three?"

"It's *your* funeral!"

I materialized one of those big, digital, drag-racer countdown clocks in the field between us. It pinged down: 0:03:00...0:02:00...0:01:00—

And then I was leaping in the air, avoiding his blinding, hypersonic blast and, simultaneously, launching the exact same sort of blast back at him out of my "hand gun."

When I landed, his discharge had scorched its way across the field behind me, setting afire some cornstalks and taking a nick out of the crown of a hill before it ripped its way into outer space.

My blast, on the other hand, had punched a ten-foot-wide, mile-deep, smoking hole in the ground right where he'd been standing.

"Anybody smell pork chops?" I asked the gawking henchbeasts in my best John Wayne impersonation. "Or is that charbroiled monkey?"

They scattered back into the forest like terrified bunny rabbits.

Chapter 69

I TURNED DANA back into herself, materialized the rest of the gang, and then—with Dad's electronic countermeasures installed in the van so that Number 5 couldn't, as far as we knew, spy on us—we proceeded to put the finishing touches on a 3-D battle map of the Wiggers' farm.

Judging from our satellite photos, the property had changed a lot over the past month.

The farmhouse and barns had been joined together by a number of alien-constructed domes, generating plants, and oblong outbuildings. And dozens of new ponds pockmarked the former corn and sorghum fields.

"Nursery ponds," said Dana.

"Looks that way," I said. "It'd be hard to raise a million little Number 5s without a habitat similar to that of his home planet."

"Check out *this* footage," said Joe, hitting a button that superimposed video images onto the map.

Hundreds upon hundreds of human forms were staggering through the fields, zombie-like in every way, except that every single one was a pregnant woman, and all were watching cell phones, iPods, or PDAs—transfixed as if engrossed in the last few minutes of an episode of *24*.

With the sort of seamless choreography you'd see in an automated factory, they split into groups and moved toward the ponds. One by one, and turn by turn, they wandered into the water, deposited the wriggling contents of their stomachs, waded back out, took another can of "caviar," and headed back to town.

And then an alarm went off. Somebody was approaching the van.

Chapter 70

"HUMANS," SAID WILLY, examining the monitor. "Lots of them."

We looked out the front and saw masses of Holliswood residents streaming toward the Wiggers' farm. They were parting around the van and staggering, barely alert, intent only on moving forward, their faces inches away from the cell phones, BlackBerries, and portable game platforms they carried.

"Holy Close Encounters of the Weird Kind," said Joe. "But these ones aren't pregnant. So what gives?"

"Well, I doubt the aliens dug all those ponds themselves. So maybe these ones are coming to do some free manual labor. That, or maybe they're coming to get filmed," said Dana.

"And then melted," added Emma.

"All right," I said. "I think it's about time we went and had a talk with Number 5."

Chapter 71

WE DROVE THE van up the poplar-lined, heavily rutted driveway and parked on the gravel by the main barn, just opposite the house.

"Lock and load, guys," Willy said as we leaped out of the van.

We closed in on the farmhouse, tree by tree, bush by bush, moving so stealthily that nobody would have heard us over the gentle breeze and chirping birds.

"Where's the welcoming committee?" signaled Joe in American Sign Language—one of thirty human languages we're fluent in—as we reached the front porch. "I mean, do we have to go up and ring the doorbell?!"

Just then, the birds stopped singing and, in unison, chirped the three tones from those NBC Peacock station-identification interludes. And then the massive barn doors swung open to reveal a JumboTron-sized video screen.

"Greetings and salutations to you and your imaginary friends, young Alien Hunter," said Number 5 from the screen. He was carrying a pitchfork and wearing a straw hat and oversized overalls—if you can imagine a creature with no legs in overalls—standing in front of a backdrop curtain patterned with a *Milky Way Hillbillies* logo.

"We'll see who's so imaginary," said Willy, attempting to storm forward as Emma and Dana held him back, "when my boot comes down on your *slimy head!*"

Number 5 ignored the outburst. "In fact, I'm honored you've come. I knew your mom and your dad—back before they got turned into crispy critters, I mean—so I have a good idea of what an upstanding young Alien Hunter you must be. You know, I may even have some footage of them around here someplace."

That was weird. I mean, obviously he hadn't arrived on Earth till long after my parents were dead, but maybe there was some chance he'd crossed paths with them when they'd been on assignment in the Andromeda galaxy, or someplace before they'd come to protect Earth...

How cool would it be to see them on film? Of course, I have my memories, and my memories—even from back when I was three, when The Prayer took their lives—are pretty good. But what if he really did have some footage of them? Maybe after I killed him, I'd go looking through his archives, just in case.

"Daniel," said Dana, "you're gaping like you're a fish. Snap out of it."

I shook my head and forced my mind through a focusing exercise Dad had taught me during my aikido training. She was right—Number 5 was obviously messing with my head.

"Sure," he went on, "I think I may have even posted them online. Here, I'll text you the YouTube link."

"I didn't bring my cell phone. It's not like I haven't figured out your infiltration techniques, Fivey."

"Well, where can I send an e-mail?"

"Try I-H-eight-F-I-S-H-at-gmail-dot-com."

He held up his Sidekick, showing me the screen and the "message sent" dialog box.

"So you've really never seen it?" he asked.

I raised an eyebrow at him.

"The scene where Number 1 killed your parents? You didn't know I was there, filming the whole thing?"

Chapter 72

"NOW I *KNOW* you're lying," I said. "I was *there* when my parents were killed."

"Sure. But were you upstairs with me and Number 1? Or were you down in the basement, playing with your toys?"

How could he have known that?

"You had no idea I was up there filming, did you? That surprises me. You know, out on the Extranet—the Outer World's version of the Internet—that clip has had more than *thirty-five trillion* downloads."

It simply wasn't possible. I'd relived that moment a thousand times. There had only been Number 1's and my parents' voices.

And in the end, there'd been nobody upstairs with my parents' bodies. I mean, I hadn't actually seen them killed, but...

"It's very moving," he said. "The part where your mom cries like a little girl is pure emotion, but my personal favorite scene is where your dad begs Number 1 for his life. *'Oh, Mr. Prayer, please, I can get you money, I can help you, just don't hurt my fa-fa-family, oh puh-lease!'*"

"Dude, that's low," said Willy, cracking his knuckles.

"Yes, perhaps that necklace of your mom's you're wearing will dispel any lingering doubts you may have. You do know it was hers, don't you? That footage where you recognized it and started crying is priceless. Just priceless!"

Had the necklace really been a plant, a setup? Had he even filmed my reaction to it...was that even possible?

"So," he went on, "it's starting to dawn on you, isn't it?"

It was no secret that Alparians wore elephant pendants. It was probably just an elaborate hoax meant to distract me, get under my skin, cause me to make mistakes—

"And, look!" he said, pulling out a necklace from behind the bib of his overalls... "We're *twins!* Do you recognize it? It was your father's, of course. Number 1 usually collects them for his trophy case, but this time he knew they'd make great props and let me borrow them. Once he was done spitting on their corpses, that is."

My mind was reeling, and I winced as I resisted throwing everything I had at the flat-screen display—but I knew that was exactly what Number 5 wanted. He was just trying to keep me from thinking rationally. There was no way he'd been in that farmhouse twelve years ago. The necklaces had to have been manufactured. And any film he showed me of my parents would turn out to be a computer-generated fake.

"Look, Daniel—may I call you Daniel? I'm first and foremost a business creature, so let's do ourselves a favor and adhere to the negotiating process here. Remember how it works? First we state our goals, and then we start working toward a deal, a compromise. So, you see, for my part, I want to create the most popular reality show of all time. Which conflicts, wouldn't you say, with your stated purpose of wanting to *exterminate me and my crew*."

"Actually," I said, somehow keeping my game face on, "you have it wrong. All I'm looking for is some information."

He nodded his fat, slimy head and gestured for me to elaborate.

"All I want to know is exactly what you want with all the people of Holliswood."

"Well, Daniel, it's just that they're as entertaining as heck." He laughed. "Of course, it doesn't hurt that they're good little workers—dumb, loyal, coachable....Did you know they created nearly thirty acres of new ponds here at the farm in just under a month? Unfortunately, there were a couple of accidents along the way. They aren't the most resilient species in the world. If I had a nickel for every bulldozer-related fatality this week..."

He chuckled to himself. "Anyhow, it's a shame we had to lose any, but I assure you we were able to recycle their remains—just as we will with the rest of them after each episode. It turns out that on top of everything else they make wonderful fertilizer. And did I mention the women are *perfect* incubators?"

Dana didn't let that one go without a response. I just wish she'd tried using words first.

Chapter 73

WITH AN ARM that would have turned Roger Clemens green with envy, Dana fired a rock straight between Number 5's eyes on the display. Sparks flew everywhere, and the screen quickly went dark.

"I think you just voided his Best Buy warranty," said Joe.

"There are too many televisions on this planet anyhow," said Emma, patting Dana on the shoulder.

There was a laugh behind us that sounded like Jell-O being liquefied in a Cuisinart. We turned to see Number 5 hovering at the end of the wraparound porch.

Absolutely live and in the flesh for the first time.

"Woo-hoo! You're a hot-tempered little product of Daniel's imagination, aren't you? Can I interest you in some caviar?"

That got the rest of the gang charging at him, but to little effect. He'd thrown some sort of crackling field of electricity around himself, and he laughed as if he were getting tickled as they bumped into the invisible barrier and fell back flat on their butts.

It shouldn't have come as any great surprise that number five on The List of Alien Outlaws on Terra Firma was not going to be taken down in hand-to-hand combat, but my friends continued to take out their frustrations on his force field—leaping, charging, punching, kicking…and always ending up flat on their backs as they failed to find a gap in his electromagnetic defenses.

Meanwhile, I watched my fish-faced foe as closely as I could—and I can watch things pretty closely.

I monitored his sweat, the rhythm of his breathing, his pulse, the slime oozing from the pores on his belly, the contractions of the suckers on his tentacles, the shape of his slimy nostrils…and, other than almost getting sick at how truly disgusting he was, almost right away I noticed something significant—a "tell," as a poker player might say of his opponent—his eyes *never* blinked.

I zoomed in my vision to about 128:1 and quickly understood why. His eyes were held open by very thin, transparent data screens that would be entirely invisible to the human eye, but I could see they were feeding him images, text, and data. It was kind of like one of those heads-up displays in a fighter pilot's helmet; only, of course, in Number 5's case, the wiring was *inside* his body.

But I didn't have time to think about it much right then.

"Thanks for keeping him distracted, guys," I said to my friends and hoped they would forgive me as I dematerialized their trigger-happy selves.

"You should have let them keep it up," Number 5 said, still laughing. "I could have gone all day."

"I was starting to get that impression," I said, gloomily.

"Oh, don't take it so hard," he said. "Can I help it if I'm *bee-oo-tee-ful* and completely *invincible* too?"

Chapter 74

BECAUSE IT HAS been scientifically determined that smiling aliens are much less likely than scowling ones to attack violently, I decided to try a charm offensive.

"Boy," I said, still playing up my disappointment, "you really *are* powerful, aren't you?"

"Let's just say I could provide power to all of New York City for, oh, a couple of *decades*. But let's not get technical. The important thing is that we're candid with each other."

"Candid?"

"Yes, young Alien Hunter. You may have had some occasional luck with my fellow List members, but don't bother trying out for any of my interstellar casting calls. Your acting skills are *atrocious*. You meant to distract me with flattery? Do you think this is my first planetary invasion?"

He laughed mockingly and went on. "I can practically

hear the gears grinding under that haircut of yours. Which is truly awful, I must say. Who was your inspiration for it anyhow—Cookie Monster?"

"That really hurts coming from a bloated swamp creature like you."

He chuckled. "Yes, I long ago realized my place is behind—not in front of—the camera. But I'm curious to see what else you have on your mind. I suspect you were looking for some sort of weakness in me, a chink in my proverbial force field. And judging from that smug look that keeps crossing your face, I expect you think you found something. So, tell me, what do you think it is? What's my Achilles' heel?"

"A weakness in *you*, the galvanic director of such intergalactic hits as *Desert Planet Booty Call* and *Shocking Alien Crime Scenes*? Not a chance. We're obviously no match for each other, so...I guess I'll be going now."

"Not so fast, you deluded little creep. You think I'd actually let you leave? Just like that? I wasn't planning on doing this just yet, but it's nothing we can't work around in postproduction. Roll cameras!" he yelled at the alien film crews that had been assembling in the yard.

"No, *really*," I said, "I'll see you *later*." And, with that, I transformed myself into a common house mosquito.

Chapter 75

NUMBER 5 BLINKED despite the hardware in his eyes. He must have thought I'd teleported myself away.

"How'd he *do* that?!" he screamed in frustration at the film crew. He yanked the railing off the side of the porch and sent it sailing through the air at them, causing them to briefly scatter.

"Gu-uh!!" he said in frustration and put his tentacles up over his head. "And where's Number 21? He was supposed to be back by now. Somebody find him!"

As Number 5 spoke, I carefully flew up to his face, landed on his nose, and jabbed my itchy, needle-like snout into it.

"Gah! Bugs!" he shouted, and as he swatted his tentacle down to crush me, I somehow overcame the nauseating taste of his putrid fish blood, grabbed onto his face with all my strength, and transformed myself into a hedgehog.

"Ahhh!" he yelled as my spines penetrated his tender flesh.

I turned myself back into human form and laughed in his face, briefly, as he got over his surprise.

"I know where Number 21 is, by the way," I revealed. "He's, um, excuse me" — I turned to spit the taste of Number 5 out of my mouth — "the latest addition to *crossed-out entries on The List*."

Number 5 gaped at me as only a fish can, and then his eyes got really dark, and he began to summon an electrical charge big enough to fry me and every life-form within a hundred yards.

Focus, Daniel, focus ... the house, the house, the house ...

And all at once, I was gone.

Dad would be proud of me. I'd teleported myself back to the safety of the house, two and a half miles away.

Chapter 76

THE WOODEN LAUNDRY table was covered with holographic maps, spreadsheets, weather reports, weapon data, and, um, Gatorade and White Castle burgers.

Mom, Dad, Pork Chop, Emma, Joe, Willy, Dana, and I were going over our final plans down in the basement. Lucky was there too, but he was more interested in intercepting a hamburger than how we were going to confront Number 5 and his minions.

"So what did you learn from your face-to-face interaction with him?" Dad asked.

"The most important thing," I said, wiping ketchup from my chin, "was that he never blinks."

"So?" asked Joe. "He never smells good, either."

"Electrical implants," I explained. "He has data screens on his eyes."

"Ahh," said Dad. "Very, very good, Daniel. You do show some promise as an Alien Hunter. . . . Not much, but some," he added with a twinkle in his eye.

"No, he doesn't," said Pork Chop. "The only thing he shows promise at is in his quest to become certified as the most annoying brother in the universe."

"That may be," said Dad, "but Daniel's discovered that Number 5 has wet wiring."

"Wet wiring? What are you boys talking about?" asked Mom.

"Number 5's powers—his ability to broadcast himself to electronic devices, to snoop around in remote wiring, to see out of television screens, etcetera, is doubtless being augmented—if not entirely enabled—by a surgically implanted computer system *in his body*."

"So, he's, like, bionic?" asked Willy.

"Like the Six Million Dollar Alien," said Joe around a mouthful of fries.

"Sort of, only what he's got would cost more like six *trillion* dollars. Not to mention that he's implanting this same kind of wiring in the hordes of alien progeny he's breeding on Earth," I commented, remembering the "alien fishnet stocking" Joe and I had observed earlier.

"So now that you've figured all that out, what good does it do us?" asked Mom.

"Well, er—," Dad fumbled for the right way to say it.

"Probably none at all," I finished for him, dropping my head.

Just then we heard a roar and rumble overhead, and we ran upstairs to see what had happened. Through the driving rain, we could see that the streetlights were out and that the neighborhood had gone completely dark.

Chapter 77

DO YOU EVER roll down the window and stick your head out when you're on the highway doing, like, sixty-five miles per hour in a downpour? You absolutely shouldn't—I mean, it's not safe—but that's what it felt like the second we stepped outside the house.

We could barely see a dozen feet in front of us, even with the lightning going off every fifteen seconds. And the thunder made it seem like we had wandered into the middle of a battlefield. The power was out all over Holliswood.

"Why are you carrying that?!" Dana yelled to me over the noise of the storm.

I was clutching a sixteen-foot copper chain and waving it around in the air above me.

"Science experiment!" I yelled, and promptly got hit by

a lightning bolt so powerful it must have flipped me thirty feet into the air and dropped me on my back.

At least that's what it felt like when I regained consciousness. My friends had dragged me into the van, and we were evidently driving on a highway.

"Are you crazy?!" asked Dana as my eyes fluttered open.

"Um, maybe," I said, sitting up. My mouth tasted like I'd been eating match heads. "Are we almost there?" I asked over the noise of the struggling windshield wipers and the hail pelting the metal roof of the van.

"Almost, dear," said Mom. "Don't tell me you need a bathroom break already?"

"Maybe if there's a doctor in the bathroom, sure," I said. Boy, did I feel terrible. But I had to let myself get struck. Just to make sure I could handle it.

"Hey," I said, suddenly realizing somebody was missing. "Where's Emma?"

"She just made us drop her off a little ways back. She wouldn't tell us why, but we figure she was going to check in on the animals at the SPCA. Anyhow, she said you'd understand."

I didn't know exactly what she was up to, but I had a hunch.

Chapter 78

THE STORM WAS weakening by the time we got to the farm, which was shrouded in darkness.

"Maybe they're gone," said Dana, as we peered out the windshield at the farmhouse.

"I don't think so," I said. "The power's out here just like it is in the rest of Holliswood. And that's precisely why I wanted to come here while the storm was still raging," I said. "With the electricity out, that should mean Number 5 won't be able to tap into the cell phone towers and other circuits to figure out where we are. And that means maybe, just maybe, we'll be able to surprise him."

"Um," said Willy, staring at the abandoned-looking farmhouse. "I mean, it's great that he might not be able to find us, but exactly how are we going to find *him*?"

"Joe's going to take care of that end of things. There's no way an alien that big and stinky can hide from the van's sensors. Any luck back there, Joe?"

"There's no sign of him—or any of the aliens—anywhere. Maybe they *did* go off someplace."

"It's not possible. I mean, they weren't ready to start the film yet. And their entire breeding operation's based here. They couldn't have picked up and left just like that..."

"The equipment's not picking anything up is all I know," said Joe.

"Maybe it's busted," said Willy, looking over Joe's shoulder with the rest of us. Everything seemed to be working, but maybe he'd forgotten to do something. It certainly was surprising that we weren't detecting any aliens whatsoever.

"Um, Daniel?" asked Dana.

"What, Dana?"

"Why are we hovering?"

"What?"

"Why is the van *hovering fifty feet in the air?*"

"What?!" I said, spinning around and spotting the wet upper branches of a maple tree through the windshield.

"Yeah, and why is there that blue glow all around us?" asked Joe.

I slid open the side door and looked down. And there, his tentacles extended toward us and pulsing blue with crackling electricity, was Number 5.

"Hello, young Alien Hunter," he said. He was no jolly Santa this time around. "Want to come down?"

I nodded wordlessly and instantly wished I hadn't.

"Hang on tight, everybody!" I yelled, as we plunged toward the earth.

Chapter 79

THE VAN SMASHED into the ground like a badly made toy—but, fortunately, one with state-of-the-art air bags, and a couple of pretty tough alien-fighters inside.

Still, we were pretty dazed as we crawled from the wreckage.

"Yeah, I think your sensors weren't working quite right, Joe," said Dana as she picked windshield glass from her hair and looked warily over toward Number 5. He was floating toward us, surrounded by a buzzing sphere of blue electricity.

"Um, right," I said as the hairs on my head—wet as they were—stood up under the force of his static charge.

"You *killed* him," he said, stopping about a dozen yards away.

"Number 21, you mean?" I said. "Well, he was trying to kill *me*, you know."

"We'd worked together for nearly three decades," Number 5 told me, scowling at me like I was an unwanted bug. "He was my right hand. And you destroyed that."

As if to echo the point, he raised his left tentacle straight in the air. A dozen stadium-style floodlights lit up the farm, and we could see that hundreds of aliens, each holding an alien weapon, had formed an enormous circle around us.

Their ranks were tight and unbroken, except for a few rain-soaked, muddy humans pushing through here and there, staggering, zombie-like, back in the general direction of town. I guessed that with Number 5 off the air during the thunderstorm, they had been returning to their homes.

"Oh, no, you don't!" yelled Number 5 in their general direction. "Back to work!"

Their cell phones and other handhelds began to ring and vibrate, and they predictably answered the devices and turned back to the fields from which they had come.

"I'm not done with any of you yet!" ranted Number 5. "And when I am, you'll know it! I'm not the universe's premiere producer of *end*ertainment for letting my actors just fade away!"

Chapter 80

"PRETTY IMPRESSIVE, NUMBER 5," I admitted, "but check this out."

I proceeded to make a cell phone ringtone all my own, consisting of the first few bars of Blondie's "Hanging on the Telephone."

"Wow, I'm *so* impressed," scoffed Number 5. "You have imaginary friends *and* you're a mimic. I should take you to a party sometime."

But then the humans' cell phones began ringing all over the farm with the same tone.

And guess who was on the line?

"People of Holliswood," I announced. "You have fallen victim to an alien invader who has been controlling your thoughts and actions through electronic devices. This is why some of you are at a farm digging ponds in the middle of a rainstorm.

"This is why the fire department is missing. This is why your children have been rehearsing a massive, alien-inspired version of *High School Musical*. And this is why you periodically find yourself doing very silly dances and musical routines for no apparent reason."

I glanced over at Number 5. He looked like he was about to explode with rage—which, I reminded myself, was just what I wanted.

Chapter 81

"I AM NOW going to ask you all to return to your homes and your normal lives," I told the citizens of Holliswood authoritatively. "But, first, I'd like you to do one last dance to show our appreciation for our alien VIP. I call it 'The Number 5,' and it goes like this—"

And then, to the jangly beats of Sissy Bar's "Space Klown," everybody in broadcast range began puffing out their cheeks, wiggling their fingers at the sides of their mouths like catfish whiskers, and swishing their butts back and forth, just like Number 5 did when he hovered around.

My gang all thought it was hilarious, and I even saw a couple aliens snickering.

Number 5, meantime, was gathering so much anger-filled energy that every hair on my body was standing on end.

"You see," I said to him in as confident a tone as I could

muster, "although I never had any doubt you'd come into this universe as an electronically gifted fish, I was totally stumped about how it was you were able to so easily broadcast yourself into electronic devices.

"I mean, I knew you'd taken over the television studio, and the broadcast substation, and the cell phone towers...but that didn't explain it. It was clear you were actually living inside the network, but how you were able to do that, well, that was the real mystery. At least until I noticed that you never blinked.

"Which led to me notice your impressive eye implants and all that crazy wiring that you must have had surgically placed inside you. I mean, that's some high-tech stuff!"

The scowl on Number 5's face was getting even uglier, if that's possible.

"And then I remembered seeing all those junior-sized neural nets in your transport containers, and I already knew you were reproducing yourself at an alarming rate—with your 'caviar' project and the ponds and all—and that must have been so you could run this program on a truly massive, planetwide scale. I mean, you don't strike me as the kind of guy who'd be into fatherhood for the pure joy of parenting."

"Well, that's all very clever," he said, smiling suddenly. "But you're still only seeing a small part of the puzzle. And the bigger piece contains the part that's about to fry your skinny little butt."

Chapter 82

TIME WAS DRAWING short, so I did another minibroadcast to the townspeople to stop their "Number 5" dance: "Thank you for that fine performance! Now, people of Holliswood, please return to your homes. A brand-new episode of *The Simpsons* is on tonight!"

"Shoot to kill any human attempting to leave the premises!" yelled Number 5 to his troops.

The humans within earshot all turned and looked at me apprehensively as hundreds of alien rifles aimed at their heads and chests.

"And bring me the McGillicutties!" their evil director commanded. "Now!"

I couldn't help but gasp. How could he have known about Judy? I'd taken every precaution...

The circle of aliens parted on one side, and Judy and her

parents were ushered through as Soul Hooligan's "Stoop Kid" began playing on speakers all over the farm.

"Do the dance!" he yelled at them, and, sure enough, Judy and her parents began doing a Soul Train–style showcase. My stomach, heart, and every other organ in my body dropped like they'd just fallen off a bridge.

"Not only will they *dance* at a word from me," said Number 5, laughing, "but they will *die,* too. So just give me a single reason, you little punk, and the next time you two want to go out for ice cream, this young woman will be numbered among your other *imaginary friends.*"

Chapter 83

IT PROBABLY WASN'T my brightest move ever, but what choice did I have?

"Let them go, Number 5," I said, aiming my hand like a gun at Number 5's flabby, slime-covered belly, just as I had with Number 21. "And I mean *right now,* or my friends and I will spend the next ten minutes wiping you and your minions off the face of the Earth."

"Oh, sure," he said, snorting even harder. "Are you guys getting all this?" he asked the circling film crews, rhetorically. "I just *knew* you were going to rise to the occasion, Alien Hunter. You've got a lot of substandard qualities I'm not going to miss, but nobody can fault your comic timing. I mean, here I am completely in control of the situation and you—what, are you going to shoot your fingernail at me?"

"Drop your cell phones, go home, and wait for us," I said to the McGillicutties.

"Ah-ah-ah," snickered Number 5, so amused that he didn't even try to stop Judy and her parents as they nervously threaded their way through the alien hordes toward town. He dabbed at his eyes with a handkerchief and turned to regard me, my friends, and my family.

"Right," he said. "So shall we do the climactic battle scene now, or do you want to go see Hair and Makeup first?"

"Very funny," I said, signaling to my friends to attack—and simultaneously unleashing a thunderous blast from my hand of the exact sort that killed Number 21.

Number 5 deflected the blast with a lightning bolt of his own, but at least I'd temporarily wiped the smile off his face. He even looked a little apprehensive as he glanced at my friends, who were now charging into his alien hordes like a bunch of berserk ninjas. Everybody but Emma, that is, who still hadn't returned.

But I couldn't worry about her now.

The battle was on.

Chapter 84

AT FIRST WE held our own. The others were laying down every martial arts trick in the book and pushing the alien scum back away from the crumpled van while I managed to keep Number 5 on the defensive—forcing him to concentrate his attention on me.

But the tide quickly began to turn. Three thousand to seven aren't good odds, no matter how you look at it.

Especially when one of the three thousand is number five on The List of Alien Outlaws on Terra Firma, and you've quickly come to discover that you have once again underestimated his powers.

Like not realizing he has the ability to adjust the electromagnetic properties of the zipper on your motorcycle jacket so that he can zip it up over your head and you can't see until you forcibly rip the thing off—just in time to see him shoot a couple thousand volts of electricity at you...

Good thing I know how to duck. Fast.

"Had enough, Alien Hunter?" he asked, smiling once again. "Want to stretch out your last seconds on Earth? I tell you what—if you do a little dance for us, maybe I'll grant you a brief respite to put on some new shoes. I can't say I've ever sensed much rhythm in you, but I bet our alien audience would love to see you do some clog dancing."

Just then a random blaster shot caught Joe in the shoulder and spun him around like a rag doll. Dana quickly dragged him to cover and got to work bandaging him up while Pork Chop and Mom gave me looks of pleading desperation.

I knew we couldn't last much longer—there were just too many of them, and I was having too much trouble with Number 5 to be able to help the others.

"You win," I said, lowering my arm.

"Surrender?" he said.

"We surrender," I said, lowering my head in shame and signaling to my friends and family to step back.

Maybe I'll still figure something out, I thought, trying to console myself.

"Ah-ah-ah!" he laughed and signaled to his troops to let up.

"Don't worry," he said, as the noise of the battle abated. "Under the circumstances, you've made the best decision you possibly could have, and I promise that your final minutes will be appreciated by trillions and trillions of aliens around the universe.

"Really," he went on, "when you think about it, what's a little humiliation and pain on your part when you'll be bringing laughter to at least half the known universe? Surely you know that old expression: 'The needs of the many outweigh the needs of the few'...or..."

His voice trailed off. Now that the melee had stopped, he and the rest of us could hear something very strange—a sort of howling, baying noise, like an enormous fox hunt, and then an unearthly roar.

We both looked over, and there to our west, cresting the hill, was an enormous, barking, snarling pack of mutts—big ones, small ones, brown ones, black ones, white ones, gray ones—racing toward the farm.

And that ant-lion that I'd rebrainwashed to hate aliens was at the head of the pack!

I also spotted, bringing up the rear—and running pretty hard to keep up—two human figures: Emma and a slightly taller one with gray hair whom I quickly recognized as the woman from the pound, the one who reminded me of my grandmother.

And then, like something out of a movie, there was a huge thunderclap and a rush of wind and rain.

The storm was picking up again.

Chapter 85

I QUICKLY DETERMINED that I wasn't going to get a better chance than this, so I secretly signaled to my friends to be ready to rejoin the battle and cleared my throat.

"Um, Number 5?" I asked as he waved at his troops to go meet the intruders and then turned his mildly perplexed fish face back to me.

"Before that dance you want me to do," I said, "can I just see that necklace of my dad's? It means a lot to me, and I just want to touch it."

Number 5 rolled his eyes. "You do have some sense for good drama, you bad-haired little twerp," he said. "Sure, that sounds cinematic enough. The orphan communes with his dead father's keepsake. Come on over and have a look. Maybe we can even have a little good-bye hug, you and I," he said, stretching his tentacles wide.

I walked up to him, knowing full well that if I tried any tricks, he was summoning enough electricity to crisp me up worse than a chicken nugget left in a microwave for twenty-five minutes. At full power.

He offered me the necklace, and I took off the one I was wearing—my mother's, he'd have us believe—and twined them together as the camera crews circled for close-up shots of the bittersweet symbolism.

And then, as the tears started to course down my cheeks, I accepted Number 5's embrace.

I realized it was entirely possible he was going to fry me right then and there, but I suspected his love of drama was going to give me at least a few more moments.

There was a growing electrical charge in the clouds overhead, and when I sensed it had reached the critical level, I freed my arm from his smothering hug and hoisted the necklaces high up into the air.

Alien Hunter science-geek fact number 45: silver is one of the best conductors of electricity in the known universe. And there's almost nothing lightning loves better.

The bolt that coursed down into my arm and met Number 5's own electrical reserves must have been more than a gigavolt, and it did just what I'd been hoping it would—it overloaded and totally *fried* his circuits.

You see, while his alien wiring had been designed to handle vast quantities of electricity, it was meant to handle it coming from the *inside*, not the *outside*.

The scream he let out almost made me feel bad for him, and the smell made me feel bad, period. All that raw electricity lit up his internal circuits like toaster wire and basically cooked him up like a three-hundred-pound platter of Cajun-style catfish.

"Disgusting!" I could hear Dana saying in the distance. I stared at Number 5's remains—just a mess of overdone fish and melted wiring—and, dazed as I was, aimed a sheepish smile in her direction.

Then I looked down—the necklaces had melted into a silver puddle of slag in the palm of my hand. Now I would never be able to prove they hadn't been my parents'.

"Ew!!" Dana exclaimed. She wasn't reacting to Number 5's remains after all. She was staring off at the alien army, which was suddenly exploding in geysers of gore. Through the storm, we could see bodies of aliens literally getting mowed down as the ant-lion and his new dog friends made short work of their terrified prey. Remember what I told you about dogs who smell bad aliens?

Needless to say, even as numerous as the aliens were, with the help of our animal friends—and with Number 5 safely out of the picture—the tide quickly turned back in our favor.

Chapter 86

DOGS AREN'T JUST a man's best friend. As it turns out, they're an Alien Hunter's best friend too. They really made all the difference when it came to wiping out Number 5's army. It even crossed my mind to adopt that ant-lion as a pet—and as a plan B for my next alien confrontation.

Dana and I were driving back into town to get Lucky from the house, and I was noticing that despite all that had happened recently, every single home was alight with the flickering blue glow of TVs and computer monitors.

"You'd think so soon after discovering the worst possible perils of electronic media, these people would chill out with all their TVs and computers and whatnot," I commented.

"Yeah," said Dana from her console in the back of the van. "And they all seem to be watching the exact same thing. Here, I'm patching it in—"

"What is it?" I asked.

"Um. We have a small problem."

"What sort of problem?"

"Well, you know how you killed Number 5?"

"Uh-huh."

"Well, you didn't quite get *all* of him."

I slammed on the brakes. "Are you *kidding?* You mean his charbroiled skeleton came back to *life?*" No way was I ready for another fish fry. I was totally wiped.

"No, it's more like his *virtual* self came back to life. It's like he's turned himself into a bunch of little computer programs on every device he ever touched...like they're all infected with a little piece of his um, personality."

I groaned. And just when I thought it couldn't get any worse, Dana continued.

"Right now he's rejoining all these little pieces and making himself into one very big, powerful dude. And, in fact, it looks like right now he's busy trying to hack his way through to a satellite uplink station."

This was bad. This was *very* bad. "Which means," I began as it dawned on me, "he's either trying to reconnect with the wider world here on Earth, so he can infect it too...or maybe he's going to broadcast into space to summon reinforcements."

"So this must have been his contingency plan. He probably didn't mean for you to fry him up like a catfish po' boy, but he had a backup plan in case you did..."

I banged my forehead against the steering wheel. Again. And again.

"What?!" asked Dana.

I sat up and turned to her. "I'd been thinking all along that he'd had that computer hardware put inside him as a sort of implant, you know, to enhance his powers. But maybe I had it backwards. Maybe Number 5 isn't an alien electric catfish at all but a computer program that *took over* an alien electric catfish."

"In other words, he was a computer program first and a catfish second, not a catfish first and a computer program second." I nodded, and Dana continued along the same lines of what I was thinking. "So maybe this isn't really much of a setback for him at all, in that case. Maybe he just needs to find another host, and he's back in business. Maybe he even *wanted* you to do this to him."

"Yeah, maybe we just freed him up so he can call the shots from cyberspace," I said.

"That would be bad," said Dana, and I did the only thing there was left to do.

I continued to bang my forehead on the steering wheel.

Chapter 87

TURNS OUT RACING along the highway with your buddies isn't nearly as fun in stinky old municipal dump trucks with grease-smeared windows as it is on high-performance motorcycles.

Still, we were pretty happy to be doing it. We had finally managed to confiscate *every single* electronic device in town and had loaded them into these garbage haulers.

How, you may ask? Sometimes, alien powers can't solve problems in an instant. Occasionally, there's absolutely no replacement for good old-fashioned elbow grease and determination. And in this case, a little high-tech hypnosis.

When we got to the Wiggers' farm, we took the garbage haulers out across the abandoned fields until we reached the alien breeding ponds.

Then we turned and dumped every Macintosh, Think-Pad, Dell, Gateway, Toshiba, Sony, LG, Motorola, Samsung, NEC, JVC, Magnavox, Westinghouse, GE, RCA, Sylvania, Nextel, Nintendo, Microsoft, AT&T, IBM, Lenovo, and a dozen other branded electronic devices—from walkie-talkies to microwave ovens to TiVos to Wiis to network routers—into the water.

It was pretty impressive—the sound of tons of twisting metal, breaking glass, and snapping plastic cascading down the hillside into a pond.

But the best part was when Number 5—who'd been silent till now, no doubt trying to figure out yet another escape plan—screamed like the Wicked Witch of the West when the stuff started splashing into the water.

The moment the first of those batteries, silicon chips, and transformers began sizzling and fizzling and shorting out, everything with a screen or a speaker began broadcasting his shrill, urgent-sounding plea:

"Stop! Please stop it! I'll make you famous. You can have a credit on my next show—I'll put your name right up there with mine—I'll even move the pilot episode to another planet if these stupid humans mean so much to you. St-oooo-op! Puh-uh-lease. My my-ind…I fe-eeel…di-zzzzzzzzz-eeee…D-d-d-ah-nnnn…yu-uhl?"

"Yes, Number 5?"

"I'm…gu…guh…gunna get you…for this."

"Oh, no, you're not," I said. And I opened up The List computer—on which I'd just run a very thorough virus scan—and deleted Number 5's entry.

The pond was soon bubbling and steaming with all the battery chemicals and electronic waste, and we watched as literally tons of stinky, finless, alien catfish began to float, belly-up, dead, to the surface of the pond.

Then I turned to the video camera that Joe was using to record the proceedings and did my best Ryan Seacrest impersonation: "We here at American Alien Hunter hope you've enjoyed Season Two. Please stay tuned for previews of our next adventure—right after this brief word from our sponsors."

Chapter 88

THEY SAY EVERYONE loves a parade, and I guess that's one more way I'm different. I guess I just think there's something unsettling about people putting on uniforms, walking together in a line, and having everybody come out to stare at them. Still, if only out of being gracious, I let the people of Holliswood put me atop their homecoming day float and rode along with the mayor through the middle of town and out to the civic auditorium where all of the children of Holliswood had assembled to stage their own version of *High School Musical*.

It wasn't really my cup of tea, but I will say one thing for Number 5's legacy—he left those kids with some darn good dance moves.

And then, since the whole town—minus those who

were melted by Number 5 and his goons—was there, I used some of what I'd learned of Number 5's mind-control broadcasting techniques and erased all memory of myself and the aliens from every single person...except Judy.

Chapter 89

I DROVE JUDY home on my motorcycle while everybody else was getting their bearings and wondering what the heck they were all doing at the civic auditorium in the middle of the day.

"You study hard with your folks, okay, Judy?"

We were standing on her porch exchanging good-byes. It was a beautiful June day. The birds were chirping, the clouds were scudding, the flowers were doing their fragrance-emitting thing.

"I just can't believe you're leaving. Can't you take me with you? I'm losing my mind here with my parents and this homeschooling business."

"I know it seems like a drag, but they're good people. I can tell. And there will be life after Holliswood, I promise."

"Easy for you to say," she said.

"Well, I have been around the block a few times—"

She interrupted me with a kiss. And, as the world spun and I saw the brilliant promise of summer in her eyes, I erased her memory of me.

Chapter 90

THE GANG AND the family and I had our final council meeting at the KHAW transmission station that we had trashed in that early skirmish with Number 5's goons.

"Checklist," I said.

Emma began. "Caviar: one hundred percent confiscated and all female residents checked to ensure no alien inhabitation. Also, all dogs from the Holliswood pound safely adopted."

"Good. Willy?"

"All incubation ponds drained and all larval Number 5s converted to crop fertilizer. All battery chemicals removed from groundwater, and all electronics fully rehabilitated. Wiggers' farm restored to its pre–Number 5 condition."

"Dana?"

"All aliens imported or bred by Number 5 have been

exterminated...except for the ant-lion, which is on an interstellar freighter on its way back to its home planet."

"Mom?"

"All essential civic functions restored. Remainder of town police currently investigating multiple missing-person claims, including loss of entire fire department."

"Pork Chop?"

"Holliswood area schools back in session. New curriculum featuring effective math and science courses. English classes now including such pillars of modern literature as *Stranger in a Strange Land*."

"Excellent. Dad?"

Dad threw a circuit breaker on the recently repaired broadcast shack's wall. "Holliswood is now officially reconnected to the wider world, and the government authorities will doubtless be showing up to assist in putting the town back on its feet."

"Joe?"

"Video scrapbook has just undergone postproduction. Screening ready to commence."

I nodded, and he fired up the projector.

We watched Number 5's landing party. The attack on the fire department. The takeover of the TV station and the Wiggers' farm. Screen tests of human families being forced to dance. The *High School Musical* practice sessions at the civic auditorium, the caviar distribution, the alien nurseries, the incubation ponds...and then the scene at S-Mart where Number 21 kicked my butt, which once again got a good laugh out of everybody.

243

"That's why we watch these things," I tried to explain. "It's like a football team reviewing the highlight reels at practice."

"Yeah, but that scene's hilarious!" said Willy.

"That's nothing," said Joe, and that's when the real laughter began. Because somehow Joe had gotten the grainy black-and-white feed of me cutting my own hair in the bathroom.

"I was trying to look like Billy Joe Armstrong!" I protested as they all rolled with laughter. "You know, the lead singer of Green Day?"

"Yeah, there's plenty to learn there," said Dana, winking at me.

"Okay, gang," I said after we sat through the final battle scenes and paused a couple of times to comment on things we could have done better. "Is that everything?"

"Oh, one last report," said Joe, somberly.

I nodded for him to go on, though I couldn't think what we hadn't covered, and what would be making him look so glum.

"I'm still not certain that operational efficiencies have recovered one hundred percent at White Castle, Taco Bell, KFC, Burger King, Wendy's, McDonald's..."

"Well, I guess we can stop by and check a couple on our way out of town," I conceded.

The strength of Joe's embrace rivaled Number 5's final squeeze.

Epilogue

GROK THIS

Chapter 91

ABOUT FIVE HUNDRED miles away, I finally stopped for lunch. The place kind of reminded me of the Holliswood Diner, although the waitstaff wasn't nearly so cute.

I politely declined the waiter's suggestion—a farm-raised catfish special—and ordered a bacon cheeseburger and a milkshake. Then I set about studying The List computer.

Number 3 was a real strange sucker from what I could tell from the few low-quality images I had on file. You know that crazy science fact about how your body's 70 percent water? Well, his apparently is 70 percent *fire*.

Suddenly I detected a possible alien presence coming up behind me, and I got ready to spring into action. My first fourteen years on Earth may have contained some harrowing moments, but, until recently, they'd been pretty well spread out. I hadn't met The Prayer till I was three, and I hadn't met another top-ten baddie till just this past year...but these days it seemed I was barely getting time for a nap between serious encounters.

It was really starting to fray my nerves.

I got ready to leap out in the aisle to deliver a round-house kick at whoever was approaching.

"Don't even think about it, Daniel," said a familiar voice. It was Dad.

"I didn't summon you," I said, regaining my breath. "How'd you just show up like that?!"

"I think part of your brain must have known you needed some parental advice," he said, sliding into the booth opposite me. "At any rate, let me do my fatherly duty and point out that there's no way you should *even think* about going after Number 3."

"Yeah, well I'd go after The Prayer himself if I thought I could find him."

"Listen, son—you were lucky with Number 6. And you were *beyond* lucky with Number 5 just now. Believe me when I tell you that you won't catch any breaks next time. The law of averages doesn't allow for exceptions that big."

"Whatever you say."

"I mean it. He'll roast you up like a kebab."

And then a very bad thing happened. That grainy image of Number 3 on The List computer suddenly became crystal clear, as in 3-D high-def clear. In fact, he looked so real I moved my hands away from the keyboard out of some instinctive fear that he might reach out and burn my fingers.

But he didn't reach out of the screen; instead, he spoke

with a British-accented voice that reminded me of Anthony Hopkins from *Silence of the Lambs:* "Listen to your daddy, sonny boy. Why don't you settle down with one of your imaginary friends and go to some nice American college with A&M or A&T in the name?"

"Now just hold on a second," I said, thinking quickly to myself. This was *my* computer. And if he was trying to scare me off already, that probably meant he was worried about me. Otherwise, why should he bother?

I mean, sure, it was scary that he had been able to find me, to bypass The List's formidable security programs, to overhear a conversation with my father, and to deliver his threat just like that...but I'd been through equally surprising circumstances just a couple times before, hadn't I?

"Tell me," I said, looking at his flickering face and acting as game as I could. "An interesting statistic I came across while reading about you: did you know that you have single-handedly contributed more to global warming than the entire industrial complex of Brazil?"

His flames visibly brightened in apparent self-satisfaction.

"Yes," I went on. "Only, I'd always assumed that was a result of your flame throwing, your hundreds of acts of arson, etcetera."

I had his attention and paused for maximum effect.

"You see, what I couldn't have known, until I'd actually had a chance to speak with you, was that really it's the tremendous quantities of hot air you release when speaking that explains it."

His glow became white hot, and I could see he was about to try something, so I quickly switched off the computer.

"You're really playing with fire now, Daniel."

"Nice one, Dad," I said, wondering what it was with him and his compulsion to make bad puns in all kinds of circumstances. "So, any chance we'll be able to do a signal trace on him?"

"I'm way ahead of you," he said, looking down at some weird cell-phone-type device with long, wiggling antennas. "And your mom will probably have my hide for telling you this...but I suppose you'd figure it out on your own anyhow....Um," he said, slumping his shoulders, although I could tell he was secretly proud of me: "It looks like the signal was originating from London, England."

"Good," I said. "I'll go book a flight. I can probably be there by tomorrow."

"Or," said Dad, "if you chose to really study the top-ographic data and teleport yourself, you could—in theory—be there in a few seconds."

"Nah, I better not push my luck, right? And anyhow," I continued as the waiter arrived and gestured for me to move my laptop out of the way, "I should probably eat some dinner first."

"Good thinking," he said, eyeing my French fries.

I summoned the rest of the family and my friends, and waved for the waiter. We clearly were going to need some more food.

"Who are we going after next?" asked Willy, sliding into the booth opposite me.

"I better not be hearing any single-digit List numbers from you this evening," said Dana.

"How are the burgers here?" asked Joe, already scanning the laminated menu.

"Aren't we supposed to take the rest of the summer off like normal kids?" asked Pork Chop. "Maybe we can go to camp!"

"Can we stop by the SPCA to thank that nice gray-haired lady again for adopting Lucky?" asked Emma.

"Next time I'm going to have to cut your hair myself," said Mom, shaking her head sadly.

I must say, probably the best thing about being an Alien Hunter...is never having to be alone.

Stay tuned.
Beware of demons and druids.
And everyone else.

—Daniel

Daniel X

For more information on Daniel X go to
www.daniel-x.co.uk

Watch the skies for
Daniel X's next incredible
adventure...

Daniel X:

Demons
&
Druids

Coming in July 2010

Turn the page for
a sneak preview!

One

I BET I CAN SEE London from here, I thought.

I was, oh, maybe 150 feet in the air, above a grassy field outside a small village called Whaddon. I'd only been in England a couple of weeks, and I still had a little of that excitement that hits you when you go to a new place.

Before I had time to take a good look around from this height, though, I started to fall.

Fast.

The first of the evening stars became a blur, and the ground seemed to rush up at me faster and faster.

I could hear shouting voices, but it was impossible to tell what they were saying over the blistering wind surrounding me.

Maybe I should have been worried, but I'll admit it—I

was enjoying myself. That is, until Willy kicked me hard in the face.

Willy, Joe, Dana, Emma, and I were playing soccer. Our own version, *where I am the ball*. That is correct; I had transformed myself into the soccer ball itself.

Luckily, soccer balls don't have a lot of nerve endings, I thought as I flew forward into the air.

"And Willy controls the centered ball beautifully, shooting a pass to Joe. He takes it up the line. But—no! Dana sweeps in with a well-executed slide tackle and steals it!" Joe always liked to deliver the play-by-play, although talking about himself in the third person usually distracted him from, well, *playing*.

"Pay attention, Joe," said Willy, grimacing. "We're getting creamed by *girls*."

Even Dana, in the middle of passing me to the other end of the field, cracked up at this.

Then she kicked me pretty hard, and once again I briefly enjoyed the feeling of flying through the evening sky—until I saw Emma's *face* rushing toward me. She caught me easily on her forehead and juggled me there for a moment as she turned to the "goalposts"—two trees at the end of the field.

Then Emma bent her body back and headed me straight up in the air. Way up. I relaxed, enjoying the sensation of free fall; it's not something I get to do that often.

Below me, Dana and Willy were racing toward the goalposts.

Dana got there first, and as I came down she jumped

into the air, fell backward, spun, and sent a scorching scissor kick through the goal.

"GOOOOOAAAAAAL!" screamed Joe from the other end of the field in his best international announcer voice.

I'd known Dana's team would win (her team always did), but her powerful kick took me by surprise. I had already overshot the goalposts by at least a hundred feet. Suddenly I realized I was headed straight for the tree-lined gorge that bordered the field.

I concentrated for a second, and then I was back to being myself again, no longer a soccer ball. I grabbed an overhanging tree branch as I flew past. Dangling one-handed over the gorge, I frowned at Dana, who was trotting over, and gave a dramatic sigh.

"You did that on purpose, didn't you?" I called to her. "Tried to kick me into the briar patch."

She laughed. "Daniel, you look like a depressed orang-utan. Get down from that branch."

Before I could come up with a snappy reply, Joe's voice rang across the field. "Okay, you two, *now* can we get going? London's not going to *walk to us!* We have monsters to catch."

Two

I DROPPED DOWN from the tree and dusted myself off. You think playing soccer is dirty?

Try being the ball.

A few minutes later, the five of us were walking along an English country road. Very picturesque, I must say.

Our pickup soccer match had been a good distraction, but now it was almost eight, and night was starting to fall.

"Well, let's hoof it, guys," I said. "In a couple of hours we can find somewhere safe to camp out."

We hadn't gone far when a light from behind made us turn around.

A large vehicle was approaching. I stuck my thumb out while my friends moved back toward the shadows, ready to disappear if need be.

Fortunately they didn't have to. As it pulled up alongside me, I saw that the vehicle was a beat-up van, and probably large enough to hold ten or eleven. A tiny woman with short gray hair was behind the wheel, wearing a tweed suit that was three sizes too big for her.

She rolled down her window and peered into the darkness behind me. "Are you lost, dearies?"

Her face looked careworn, but she had smile lines around her mouth. I liked the way she looked, and I liked her spacious van even more.

I put on my best harmless-backpacking-tourist face. "I'm afraid we're stranded, ma'am. We're trying to get to London." *To catch some aliens—Number 3 to be exact.*

"Oh...Americans!" She smiled. "Well, I'm heading that way. Hop in."

Three

IT DIDN'T TAKE much to convince us. We gratefully piled in, Willy and Emma in back, Dana and me in the middle row, and Joe sprawled out in the passenger seat.

We drove in silence for about ten minutes. Joe had nodded off, and Willy and Emma were chatting in hushed, lazy voices behind me.

I normally talk with the people who pick me up, but it had been a long day. My eyes were about to close when Dana's lips brushed against my ear. Yeah, *that* woke me up.

"Have you noticed?" she whispered.

"What?" I whispered back.

"The driver's seat—it's on the left side."

"So? That's where it's supposed to be."

"Not really, Daniel. We're in England, remember? They drive on the other side."

That's a little unusual, I thought to myself. *Why would the van be American?*

And there was something else, something that had been gnawing at me since we got in. Something about what the driver was wearing. Tweed is a rough woolen fabric. It's often used for the jackets of college professors, pipe-smoking stamp collectors, and—I now remembered—outdoorsmen, such as *hunters*.

I tried to lean forward to get a better view. That's when I realized I couldn't move a muscle, couldn't even blink.

"So you've noticed, *dearie.*" The driver's voice seemed to catch in her throat, then something harsh came out, not a human sound. Not even close. "I'm a hunter. *Just. Like. You.* And I do believe I've just caught dinner!"

Four

SUDDENLY WE WERE all wide awake, even Joe, who we always joked didn't sleep — he hibernated.

"Uh-oh. I can't move, guys, not even an eyelid. This could be bad."

"Since when are you the master of understatement, Joe?" snapped Dana.

"Since when is Daniel the master of getting us caught by the bad guys?" answered Joe.

She frowned. "Touché."

"Silence!" shouted the driver in an alien rasp. It seemed all wrong: that metallic, scraping voice, coming out of that kind-looking grandmother's face.

As she said it, though, a gray, pulsating tentacle descended from the ceiling and wrapped itself around my mouth. It felt sticky, warm, and alive. Out of the corner of my eye, I could see a dozen more tentacles gagging my friends.

Dana's eyes met mine. "Daniel. What's *happening?*"

I had no idea.

I couldn't really move my head, but as my eyes scanned the walls of the van, I could see them moving, pulsating, *breathing*. The walls definitely hadn't been doing *that* before. And the roof—it was a forest of waving gray tentacles.

Now I understood why we couldn't move our bodies. The van's seats had sent out tendrils that were no thicker than rubber bands, but they were strong and enveloped our arms and legs more effectively than steel manacles could.

More than anything, the tentacles reminded me of the sea anemones I used to find in the tide pools on the Oregon coast. Unsuspecting fish that swam too close would be grabbed, stunned by the neurotoxins in the anemones' tentacles, and slowly digested.

That's what this van was, I realized suddenly. *A giant anemone.*

Five

WITH THIS DISCOMFORTING and demoralizing realization came another totally creepy thought: the driver wasn't actually driving, she was part of the alien, one of its organs. She was bait. How many hitchhikers had been picked up by this kindly looking old lady, only to become her dinner?

She — it, I should say — saw my look of understanding and horror.

"Ah, my tentacles are full of neurotoxins. Thank you for noticing." It cackled nastily. "All the better to kill you with, dearie."

I had to do something; I had to do something right now. *But what?*

The problem was I couldn't move, I couldn't create anything, I couldn't transform. I couldn't even talk, to tell my friends to break out, to run away.

"Yes, indeed. This is when the hunter becomes the hunted and then becomes tonight's repast. Just be thankful that you'll all be dead before you're digested. I'm told that the process is excruciating." Somehow this didn't come as much consolation to me.

The old woman's body began to transform now, melting into her seat. Meanwhile, a bulbous tentacle tightened around my mouth, and the interior of the van seemed to be getting smaller and smaller. *That was just claustrophobia, right?* Hey, I had to get a hold of myself.

No, the van was definitely getting smaller. Shrinking! I blinked, desperately trying to clear my mind and find a quick solution. Being squashed into mush and then digested? Not how I was planning to leave the Earth.

Up front in the van, Joe's head was shuddering as he struggled against paralysis. I could hear Emma gurgling behind me. And Dana's beautiful eyes—they were huge with fear.

The alien anemone's voice rasped again. The driver was gone, but mouths had opened up *in the walls* around us, hundreds of them. It was like listening to the worst chorus imaginable—in surround sound.

"This is for my beloved brother, Alien Hunter. It's too bad he couldn't be here to see it. Do you remember Number 40? You disintegrated him in Dallas, Texas!"

Of course I remembered, but I couldn't focus on past victories right now.

The walls and ceiling constricted yet again. *Like a giant heart beating*, I thought. The roof was pressing down hard

13

against our heads now. The van's interior had become smooth and oily; it reminded me of the inside of a stomach.

"Nice eating you..." The beast's final message trailed off in a sickening gurgle. "I'm Number 43 by the way. My brother's name was Jasper."

"I remember — may he rest in pieces!" I quipped. What else could I do?

Another powerful contraction came. The walls closed in even tighter, pushing me and Dana together — something I might have enjoyed, if we weren't both about to become meat-and-bone Jell-O pudding.

I'd never felt anything like this before. I was hurting all over, and not just physically. It was like all the terror my friends were feeling was being transmitted back to me a hundred times over. I had never gotten them into a situation this bad before; it looked like I wouldn't have the chance to get them out of it.

The walls kept closing in, bending me double. The tentacle around my throat was twisting too tight for me to even swallow. *It's over*, I thought. Everything was getting dim, and quiet, and distant. My eyes were finally squeezed shut, and I thought I might suddenly burst like a zit caught in tweezers.

And then behind the pain and the fear, I heard words way in the back of my mind.

"You still have time....you can take out Number 43. At least I think so."

I recognized the voice immediately. It was my father.

My *dead* father.

**THE WORLD ALL AROUND YOU.
LIFE AS YOU KNOW IT.
EVERYTHING YOU LOVE.
IT ALL CHANGES — NOW.**

*This is the story I was born to tell.
Read on, while you still can.*
—JAMES PATTERSON

COMING IN OCTOBER 2009

Prologue

WISTY

IT'S OVERWHELMING. A city's worth of angry faces staring at me like I'm a wicked criminal—which, I promise you, *I'm not*. The stadium is filled to capacity—*past* capacity. People are standing in the aisles, the stairwells, on the concrete ramparts, and a few extra thousand are camped out on the playing field. There are no football teams here today. They wouldn't be able to get out of the locker-room tunnels if they tried.

This total abomination is being broadcast on TV and on the Internet too. All the useless magazines are here, and the useless newspapers. Yep, I see cameramen in elevated roosts at intervals around the stadium.

There's even one of those remote-controlled cameras that runs around on wires above the field. There it is—hovering just in front of the stage, bobbing slightly in the breeze.

3

So, there are undoubtedly millions more eyes watching than I can see. But it's the ones here in the stadium that are breaking my heart. To be confronted with tens, maybe even hundreds of thousands of curious, uncaring, or at least indifferent, faces...talk about *frightening.*

And there are no moist eyes, never mind tears.

No words of protest.

No stomping feet.

No fists raised in solidarity.

No inkling that anybody's even thinking of surging forward, breaking through the security cordon, and carrying my family to safety.

Clearly, this is not a good day for us Allgoods.

In fact, as the countdown ticker flashes on the giant video screens at either end of the stadium, it's looking like this will be our *last* day.

It's a point driven home by the very tall, bald man up in the tower they've erected midfield—he looks like a cross between a Supreme Court chief justice and Ming the Merciless. I know who he is. I've actually met him. He's The One Who Is The One.

Directly behind his Oneness is a huge N.O. banner—*the New Order.*

And then the crowd begins to chant, almost sing, "The One Who Is The One! The One Who Is The One!"

Imperiously, The One raises his hand, and his hooded lackeys on the stage push us forward, at least as far as the ropes around our necks will allow.

I see my brother, Whit, handsome and brave, looking

4

down at the platform mechanism. Calculating if there's any way to jam it, some way to keep it from unlatching and dropping us to our neck-snapping deaths. Wondering if there's some last-minute way out of this.

I see my mother crying quietly. Not for herself, of course, but for Whit and me.

I see my father, his tall frame stooped with resignation, but smiling at me and my brother—trying to keep our spirits up, reminding us that there's no point in being miserable in our last moments on this planet.

But I'm getting ahead of myself. I'm supposed to be providing an *introduction* here, not the details of our public *execution*.

So let's go back a bit....

BY ORDER OF THE NEW ORDER,

and the Great Wind—The One Who Is

THE ONE—

let it be known that as of

NOW, THIS MOMENT, or

TWELVE O'CLOCK MIDNIGHT,

whichever shall arrive first, following the
SWIFT TRIUMPH of The **ORDER** of the
ONES WHO PROTECT, who have obliterated the
BLIND AND DUMB FORCES of passivity and
complacency **PLAGUING** This World,
ALL CITIZENS *must, shall,* and *will* abide by

THESE THREE ORDERS for ORDER:

1. All behaviors NOT in keeping with N.O. law, logic, order, and science (including, but not limited to, theology, philosophy, the creative and dark arts, et cetera) are hereby ABOLISHED.
2. ALL persons under eighteen years of age will be evaluated for ORDER-LINESS and MUST COMPLY with the prescribed corrective actions.
3. The One Who Is THE ONE grants, appoints, decides, seizes, and executes at will. All NOT complying shall be SEIZED and/or EXECUTED.

—As declared to the One Who Writes Decrees
by THE ONE WHO IS THE ONE

One

WHIT

SOMETIMES YOU WAKE up and the world is just plain different.

The noise of a circling helicopter is what made me open my eyes. A cold, blue-white light forced its way through the blinds and flooded the living room. Almost like it was day.

But it wasn't.

I peered at the clock on the DVD player through blurry eyes: 2:10 a.m.

I became aware of a steady *drub, drub, drub*—like the sound of a heavy heartbeat. Throbbing. Pressing in. Getting closer.

What's going on?

I staggered to the window, forcing my body back to life after two hours passed out on the sofa, and peeked through the slats.

And then I stepped back and rubbed my eyes. Hard.

Because there's no way I had seen what I'd seen. And there was no way I had heard what I'd heard.

Was it really the steady, relentless footfall of hundreds of soldiers? Marching on my street in perfect unison?

My street wasn't close enough to the center of town to be on any holiday parade routes, much less to have armed men in combat fatigues coursing down it in the dead of night.

I shook my head and bounced up and down a few times kind of like I do in my warm-ups. *Wake up, Whit.* I slapped myself a couple of times for good measure. And then I looked again.

There they were. Soldiers marching down our street. Hundreds of them as clear as day, made visible by a half-dozen truck-mounted spotlights.

Just one thought was running laps inside my head: *This can't be happening. This can't be happening. This can't be happening.*

Then I remembered the elections, the new government, the ravings of my parents about the trouble the country was in, the special broadcasts on TV, the political petitions my classmates were circulating online, the heated debates between teachers at school. None of it meant anything to me until that second.

And before I could piece it all together, the vanguard of the formation stopped in front of my house.

Almost faster than I could comprehend, two armed squads detached themselves from the phalanx and sprinted across the lawn like commandos, one running around the back of the house, the other taking position in front.

I jumped back from the window. I could tell they weren't here to protect me and my family. I had to warn Mom, Dad, Wisty—

But just as I started to yell, the front door was knocked off its hinges.

Two

WISTY

IT'S QUITE HIDEOUS to get kidnapped in the dead of night, right inside your own home. It went something like this.

I awoke to the chaotic crashing of overturning furniture, quickly followed by the sounds of shattering glass, possibly some of Mom's china.

Oh, God, Whit, I thought, shaking my head sleepily. My older brother had grown four inches and gained thirty pounds of muscle in the past year. Which made him the biggest and fastest quarterback around, and, I must say, the most intimidating player on our regional high school's undefeated football team.

Off the playing field, though, Whit could be about as clumsy as your average bear — if your average bear were hopped-up on a case of Red Bull and full of himself because he could bench-press 275 and every girl in school thought he was the hunk of all hunks.

I rolled over and pulled my pillow around my head. Even before the drinking started, Whit couldn't walk through our house without knocking something over. Total bull-in-the-china-shop syndrome.

But that wasn't the real problem tonight, I knew.

Because three months ago, his girlfriend, Celia, had literally *vanished* without a trace. And by now everyone was thinking she probably would never come back. Her parents were totally messed up about it, and so was Whit. To be honest, so was I. Celia was—*is*—very pretty, smart, not conceited at all. She's this totally cool girl, even though she has money. Celia's father owns the luxury car dealership in town, and her mom is a former beauty queen. I couldn't believe something like that would happen to someone like Celia.

I heard my parents' bedroom door open and snuggled back down into my cozy, flannel-sheeted bed.

Next came Dad's booming voice, and he was as angry as I've ever heard him.

"This can't be happening! You have no right to be here. Leave our house *now!*"

I bolted upright, wide awake. Next came more crashing sounds, and I thought I heard someone moan in pain. Had Whit fallen and cracked his head? Had my dad been hurt?

Jeez, Louise, I thought, scrambling out of bed. "I'm coming, Dad! Are you all right? Dad?"

And then the nightmare to start a lifetime of nightmares truly began.

I gasped as my bedroom door crashed open. Two hulking men in dark gray uniforms burst into my room, glaring at me as if I were a fugitive terrorist cell operative.

"It's her! Wisteria Allgood!" one said, and a light bright enough to illuminate an airplane hangar obliterated the darkness.

I tried to shield my eyes as my heart kicked into overdrive. "Who are *you?!*" I asked. "What are you doing in *my freaking bedroom?*"

Witch & Wizard
In stores October 2009.

About the Authors

JAMES PATTERSON is one of the best-known and biggest-selling writers of all time. He is the author of some of the most popular series of the past decade: the Women's Murder Club, the Alex Cross novels and Maximum Ride, and he has written many other number one bestsellers including romance novels and stand-alone thrillers. He lives in Florida with his wife and son.

James is passionate about encouraging both adults and children alike to read. This has led to him forming a partnership with the National Literacy Trust, an independent, UK-based charity that changes lives through literacy.

NED RUST lives in Croton, New York, with his family. His writing has appeared in *Rolling Stone* and McSweeney's Internet Tendency.

We support

I'm proud to support the National Literacy Trust, an independent charity that changes lives through literacy.

Did you know that millions of people in the UK struggle to read and write? This means children are less likely to succeed at school and less likely to develop into confident and happy teenagers. Literacy difficulties will limit their opportunities throughout adult life.

The National Literacy Trust passionately believes that everyone has a right to the reading, writing, speaking and listening skills they need to fulfil their own and, ultimately, the nation's potential.

My own son didn't used to enjoy reading which was why I started writing children's books – reading for pleasure is an essential way to encourage children to pick up a book. The National Literacy Trust is dedicated to delivering exciting initiatives to encourage people to read and to help raise literacy levels. To find out more about the great work that they do visit their website at www.literacytrust.org.uk.

James Patterson